STEALING HER

ALEXIS ABBOTT

PATHFORGERS PUBLISHING

Get an EXCLUSIVE book, **FREE** just as a thank you for signing up for my newsletter! Plus you'll never miss a new release, cover reveal, or promotion!

http://alexisabbott.com/newsletter

I'm going to be late for class. I cannot be late for class.

I can't breathe, and the first thing I worry about is class.

A hand is around my face. A cloth is blocking my nose. My mouth. I can't see the person behind me. Panic is rising in me, and all I can think about is not being irresponsible.

The world is already so dim and eerie this time of morning, and through the veil of panic descending over me, I can just barely make out the gently waving dark arms of trees against the pale gray sky. Dawn has not even broken yet, the clouds intact before the streaking rays of sunrise could splinter the colors into a kaleidoscope above my head.

I usually love this time of day. Early, empty mornings between the last dregs of party kids trundling back to their dorms to conk out for a few hours of drooling sleep before an eight-AM math class and the soft, slow awakening of the daybreak people. The early risers and go-getters briskly jogging across campus with their enormous thermoses of stale coffee, a low-calorie power bar crumbling in their other hand.

The type-As.

The perfectionists

The late-to-bed-and-early-to-risers.

That is the caste I most neatly fit within. That is the descriptive category to which I most clearly belong. It's evidenced by every teacher report my father has ever received on my behalf. *Lila Hawthorne is a tireless worker, a brilliant student, a joy to teach.*

Sometimes, in my darkest, loneliest, most hopeless pits of despair, I replay those phrases over and over again in my mind, shouting them with a bullhorn in an attempt to drown out the low, fiendish chanting of my insecurities.

Not good enough.

Not smart enough.

Not strong enough.

Obey.

Listen.

Be quiet.

And now, I can add, not attentive enough. I never even heard the person sneak up behind me. I never saw even a shadow or heard the crunch of dull leaves beneath their shoes. Thoughts rush through my brain.

Why me?

What's happening?

I try to scream, but it's no use. The cloth muffles the sound, and the man behind me pulls me closer to him, my head pressing against his body. How tall is he? I move my head slightly, trying to feel the ridges of his form, get an understanding of how much taller he is, and I figure he has at least a foot and a half on me.

My hand lashes out, groping for his hip, but he's too fast and sidesteps me. He doesn't make a sound, not even a grunt as he moves. He's like a specter, and my world is getting dimmer.

The cloth must have something on it. Something that's making my head foggy. I don't have a lot of time. My eyes dart around, praying for a jogger or a professor to be walking nearby, but there's just the eerie stillness of the early morning.

Serenity surrounds me as a red-hot fury takes hold of me and I thrash, but my motions are weak. The drug is doing its job, slowing my body down. Slowing my mind to a crawl.

The image of my father flashes in my mind. Everything I've done to perfect myself has been to please him, to find some way to make him see something special in me. To see me at all. But no matter my good grades, no matter how many glowing reports make their way to his office, no matter how many days I wake up at 5 in the morning to get a jump on the day, he never seems to notice.

I need him to approve. I need him to love me.

No matter where I am currently falling in the crests and crashes of life, there is that one solid constant: everything I do, everything I am, every-thing I ever will be— it's all to impress him. To make my father believe that I am worth his investment. I need to be an asset. I refuse to be a liability. It's my number one fear: letting him down.

And perhaps that is why, even as the leathery, gloved hand clasps violently over my mouth and nose, closing up my airways, I am less afraid than I should be of whoever it is wielding the glove, and more afraid of what my father will think. How disappointed will he be when he finds his careless daughter has been…

Has been what?

My mind goes blank for a second, the drugs making everything so… fuzzy.

I hold my breath, trying to hold onto conscious-ness longer. How long has it been? It feels like days have passed, but something within me says it's not even been a minute. How long would the drugs take to work? Longer than my captor would want. Shorter than what I need.

My captor yanks me close, my back pressing against his taut, powerful abdominal muscles. His free arm coils around me, his enormous hand grasping my shoulder, keeping my arms pinned down. He's powerfully built, muscle upon muscle upon malice.

What does he want with me?

What does any man want with a girl like me?

Judging by what Daddy has told me, men move through this world with only two intentions: to own a woman or to break a woman.

I may only be twenty years old, but I'm more than old enough to know that he's not just being cynical. He isn't just trying to scare me straight like some childhood book of morals. He tells me the truth. I trust in him even more than I trust in myself, in my own instincts.

The gloved hand slides up on my face. All my air supply has been slashed. The stale air in my mouth tastes acrid and bitter. It tastes like death. The man jolts me from my place on the pathway. He pulls me off the trail and behind a cluster of oak trees. The branches arch down around us almost like the loving arms of a mother.

Not that I have any real idea what that might feel like. I killed my mother, or rather, my birth killed her.

I hold my breath instinctively, seizing up and trying to turn my diminutive frame into as much dead weight as possible, even as the lack of oxygen flow makes me dizzy. It's difficult now to sort out my thoughts into clear patterns. It all crisscrosses and superimposes and blends together into a mass of colorful panic, stars bursting behind my eyelids as my body weakens in the arms of my faceless captor.

Suddenly, a thought slices through the fog in my mind like a machete through the jungle green: I should scream. I should kick. I should make myself difficult to take.

It goes against all of my instincts, of course. I've always been taught to be quiet and soft and easy. A young woman should be pliable. She should be affable. Obedient. Seen and not heard. I should listen and follow, never speak up without prompting.

But surely this is different, isn't it? Surely my father would understand. He would never want me to be captured and dragged away to meet some grisly unceremonious fate in the gnarled bushes of the MIT campus. I have to fight, even though the fairer sex is never meant to fight.

Still holding my breath, I summon up every tiny shred of my strength and courage, letting my lungs seize control of what little air is left to them. I wrench away from my captor's grasp just long enough to free my lips momentarily. I gulp down a gasp of delicious, precious air and fill my chest with it, reveling in the freedom of breath.

I have to scream.

I open my mouth and tilt my head back, begging

my body to catch up and do as I say. Please. Just this once, disobey. Do not be silent. You must fight back.

Some pathetic, half-strangled disaster of a scream rips from my throat. The sound of it actually frightens me, as it more closely resembles the cry of some wild animal with its leg in a vice than anything remotely similar to human speech. It is the cry of a wounded prey animal, desperately calling for someone to rescue it before death can creep into the clearing.

My hope, what little there was, is cut short. The gloved hand shoves a fist into my mouth, aching my cheeks and making my jaw click painfully. I shudder and try my hardest to bite down on the gloved hand, but whatever material the glove is made from is more than enough to withstand my attempt. It smells of leather, and behind it, there is that softer, muted scent that misleads me into a sense of comfort. It's like cologne oil or aftershave. Something vaguely peppermint, vaguely musk. The distinctive scent of a well-groomed man.

I find myself suddenly desperate to know the shape and shadows of his face. But I can't know that. No matter how violently I try to pull away, to twist my body around and face my attacker head-on, he's too strong. He keeps me facing the tree. My eyes glance around frantically as the early morning sun gradually starts to illuminate the campus in pale gray patches between the trees. I know enough from watching true crime documentaries about kidnappings and murders that it is vital for me to memorize as much as I can of the scene unfolding all around me, of which I am the unwilling star.

But there is nothing much to take in. The campus is barren this time of day. It's the reason I'm out here in the first place. I like to go for long walks in the early morning, before the campus is overflowing with competition. I like the silence, the ominous rush of branches swaying in the breeze over my head, casting devilish shadows on the paths.

I should have known better. I should have been smarter.

Of course, it is dangerous to walk here alone during these hours. In this moment, all I can feel is anger toward myself. How could I have been so stupid? There is no one to save me. No one to even witness the attack. I'm alone. Just my captor and me and the tree.

He hastily slips that fabric between his gloved hand and my face. I'm able to catch a faint whiff of the cloth this time, and my mind goes haywire with panic. The cloth feels strangely cold and wet, but I know it isn't ice water.

It's chloroform. Of course it is. How did I not realize it sooner?

Don't breathe. Don't breathe, I remind myself. Hold your breath for as long as it takes.

But I know it's futile. If I hold my breath too

long, I will pass out. But if I give in and gasp for air, the chloroform will knock me out, too. How long will it take? How much is already in my system? There's no way out. There's no way free. I just have to acquiesce to whatever dark purpose my attacker has in mind.

I buck my body again, but it's hopeless. It's all hopeless.

The last thing I see before the stars explode to black and the world collapses in around me is the intricate texture, the jagged lines and shades of the oak tree bark millimeters from my face. Mingled with the perfume of musk, leather, chloroform, and panic is the piney scent of a forest. As my body goes limp and the curtain falls across the stage, all I can think about is how much I'm letting him down.

I'm sorry, Daddy. I tried my best.

My eyes open slowly, one at a time. I can feel my body quaking from side to side, and at first, I assume I'm having some sort of slow-motion seizure. I have no control over where I go or what I do. My legs are bound together. My arms are twisted and bound behind my back. My every muscle aches and twinges with the pain of being held in the same position for too long. I'm not sitting still, though, that I know for certain. I'm going forward somehow, and when my head lolls back, my neck too weak to hold it up, I realize that I can only catch faint, blurry glimpses of light and dark. There are no images, no treetops, no buildings, no sky to speak of. But it's not because the world has dissolved away. It's because someone has tied a blindfold around my head. I try to open my eyes, but my eyelashes just bat against the inner cloth of the blindfold uncomfortably. I close them again. There's no point. It's too tightly secured.

Besides, I have an inkling that I would not recognize my current whereabouts even if I wasn't blinded with a cloth. I have no idea how long I was knocked out.

I am so tired.

My body is weak from the chloroform, from sitting in this uncomfortable position, from being so constantly afraid.

That is one thing I've learned over the course of my life thus far: pain and fear are exhausting. The heavier the burden you carry, the more slowly you must go along. Let's just say my father has given me burden after burden to bear on my shoulders, ever since I was a child.

It's a form of love from him. He wants me to be strong. To be better than any other girl. I have to be beautiful and clever and perfect and I have to work harder than anyone else. I have to be the best, and there is no burden heavier than that one.

But perhaps it is a gift, because now, under what one would probably categorize as "extreme duress," I am not in a full-blown panic. In fact, I am trying to remain as calm as one can under such circumstances. I have to be analytical about this. I cannot see anything and I cannot move, but that leaves me with scent and sound. All I can smell is the musty cloth around my eyes and the pungent leathery scent of perhaps a recently-detailed rental vehicle. I listen intently, holding my breath, and judging from both the bumpiness of the ride and the volume of the engine's roar, it's a large vehicle. Probably a minivan or an industrial work van. I assume, because I am a captive, that the van is windowless. Or perhaps the windows are just very darkly tinted. I don't know for sure, but it seems like a fair guess.

I don't hear other cars passing by, so I guess that we're on some back road away from the prying eyes of civilization. In New England, there are lots of places that fit the bill. You can be in the center of a city and still be only a short drive from the middle of nowhere. And again, I have no clue how long I was unconscious. Minutes. Hours. Days. I could still be within a mile of the campus or I could be halfway across the continent by now. I have no way of knowing.

And I am so, so tired. I drift off to a restless, fitful sleep.

When I wake up, I hear the whine of the vehicle

engine as the van rolls to a stop, crunching over what sounds like gravel. My heart starts to pound mercilessly as the dark recent events come flooding back to me. I have to pee so badly. My stomach aches. My entire body twinges with cramps. And I can feel goosebumps poking up on my flesh as the doors of the van slide open with a scraping sound.

I try to recoil from the sound, folding myself up as small as I can manage despite the weakness of my muscles.

It's pointless.

A pair of heavy, calloused hands grab hold of me and drag me out of the back seat. I can feel the slightly cool air touch my skin. I can smell dampness. An earthy smell that reminds me of blind worms tunneling underfoot. My captor guides me without a word, my tingling feet crunching over dewy grass and muddy soil as he marches me along. The feeling slowly returns to my legs as I walk, the sensation of pins and needles nearly as torturous as the kidnapping itself.

He prods me in the small of my back and I shiver. I open my mouth to say something, only to realize there's nothing I can say. What could I do? Ask him his name? Beg for my life?

I know enough about the world to understand that no man alive wants anything good for me. Nobody but my father cares about me, and even he has a strange way of showing it. No, it's better for me now and always to simply obey without a word.

Don't cause a fuss.

Don't do anything that would cause them to hurt me.

Don't say anything that will make this worse.

In the movies, everyone always yells at the heroine to not run up the stairs, don't go with him. Always struggle. Always scream.

They don't understand that smart girls do whatever it takes to survive, and sometimes the smartest thing is to not give them a reason to hurt you.

Bide your time.

Plan to live another day. Another hour. Another minute.

I let this mysterious hulk of a man prod me along the soft, wet earth until we stopped momentarily. For a split second, I thought perhaps I should run. But I realized quickly how stupid it would be. I couldn't get very far, and besides, I had no idea where I was.

Where would I go?

What direction?

I can't approach this scattershot. My best chance for escape was at the campus, and the man who took me was too powerful for me to run from. Running now would just give him a reason to think I was going to be trouble. That he should be careful with me.

And then there'd be no escape at all.

So, I stay put and let him guide me through a creaking doorway into a place that's totally dark and smelled of rotting earth. I wrinkle my nose and cough underneath the cloth wrapped around my eyes and mouth. My captor's hands push me forward on and on, step by stumbling step, into the murky, musty darkness.

Then, without saying a word to me, he leaves me here.

I hear his footsteps retreating in the other direction. I turn slowly around to 'watch' him leave with my covered eyes. Through the thick fabric of the blindfold I can make out the faint shimmering of daylight at the entry of whatever hole he's shoved me into. I follow the vague silhouette of my kidnapper as he ducks out into the sun. The door slowly closes, shutting out the light to leave me standing hopeless and paralyzed in the penetrating dark.

I stare at the wall, my heart having finally calmed down from its galloping pace to beat a slow, even rhythm of pure resolve. This is what I have to get used to now. This is where I might have to make my home, at least for the time being.

That's what I try to tell myself. It's strange, maybe, and some might call it learned helplessness. In fact, that is the exact term my old psychology professor probably would have used on me at this point.

He was always kind of a jerk, anyway.

Pointing me out in class, calling on me to try and catch me off-guard, but I always knew the answer. I always knew what to say to keep my grade point average dangling high, high above my classmates. My father taught me that there is nothing less I can do if I want to make it in this world. If I want to succeed, I have to be the best, especially since I'm a woman and there's little I can do about that.

I never learned to be helpless, contrary to what that skeezebag of a professor tried to pin on me. I evade diagnosis. I defy categorization. It's what I have strived for my entire life— to be not only good enough, but better. Daddy expects nothing less of me, and god forbid I ever let him down, even now, locked away in this musty, dank hole in the ground.

But once I escape, he will be proud. He has to be. I've been taken, and I have no information about the who or what or where or why. It's like a puzzle, one I have to solve, and that makes it a little less scary. If it's a puzzle, it's a game.

And a game can't be scary.

I wonder what the hell this place could actually be. Some kind of post-apocalyptic bomb shelter built by some guy with equally superfluous levels of wealth and paranoia, maybe? I know the type. My father is a highly successful businessman. He moves through a world of old money and new money, all of them doggedly dedicated to collecting new shiny toys to show off and prove their worth to everyone else in the same socioeconomic class. Usually, it was a car. Or several cars, to be more exact. Orange Lamborghinis with the vertically-opening doors. Baby blue Bentleys with the creamy leather interior. A glossy Rolls-Royce Phantom with its blocky shape and seats the precise color of a Fijian sunset. Of course, they all owned houses— massive and multiple. My father has a summer house somewhere in an exclusive beachy neighborhood of Miami. I have never been there.

He prefers to keep me separated from that world. Always at arm's length, until I finally find the way to make him realize that I'm worth it.

And then, as expected there are the millionaires and billionaires who funnel their endless cash flow into less pedestrian pursuits. Instead of a glitzy car or a twenty-room mansion in Florida, they spent their fortune on daydreams and nightmares. I remember once Daddy had a friend who cornered me at a party we held at our place so he could rant and rave on and on to me about his end-of-the-world preparedness. He droned on about his bunker, his pantries upon pantries of canned goods and endless bulk-sized packages of toilet paper. It was much more difficult to pretend to be interested in that conversation than it is to sit through any number of college classes. Now I'm grateful I managed to listen to the whole conversation. Maybe that information could help me in here.

Wherever here is.

I shift uncomfortably, grimacing at the damp, musty earth underneath me. Whatever I must be sitting on right now is undoubtedly staining the hell out of my clothes. My father would have a lot to say about that if he were here. I ponder that for a brief moment: what if he turns up any second now to save me from whatever hell this is?

I realize with a sinking feeling that I would almost rather stay here longer and try to figure it out myself than let Daddy see me this way. I know the look he would give me, that furrowed-brow expression that wordlessly conveys his disappointment in me. His disgust. I am constantly working against that look. I want, just once, to make him smile.

I know he must be capable of it, right? He was married at one time— to my own mother. Surely, they used to smile sometimes. They had to have been in love at some point. Of course, I ruined all of that by being born. Maybe there was a time when Daddy was content, but never during my lifetime.

I have spent the past twenty years of my life trying to make up for killing Mom. I didn't mean to. I had to be born somehow. And yet, it's the one weight on my shoulders I could never shrug off.

Sometimes, as a kid, I wondered if I had broken him. If I was to blame for my father's quiet cruelty.

I made him this way, didn't I?

So I am forever trying to please him, to atone for the crime I committed the very day I entered this world. I deserve his anger, his disapproval. But at least there are some who don't look at me with resentment.

I have a friend. Just the one. Her name is Cassandra. We met when I became her math tutor awhile back. She's the same age as me, both of us trekking through college together, although she's not a business major like I am. She studies art and photography, kind of the creative yin to my analytical yang.

I sit up straight and rigid suddenly, a realization dawning over me.

What is going to happen to Henry?

My heart aches and I have to bite the inside of my cheek to keep the tears from rolling down my cheeks. Henry is my angel. He's a scrappy little terrier, a shaggy-haired, twelve-pound mutt I adopted from the animal shelter where I volunteer. I only started volunteering there as a means of padding out my resume— or at least that's what I tell Daddy— and I had set the hard rule for myself that I would not take home any of the animals. Growing up, I was never allowed to have a pet, and I assumed it just wasn't for me. Daddy always made it sound like such a tedious pain, having to pay for and look after a dumb little animal. He always reasoned that it was silly to spend money and time on a dog when you could be buying a motorcycle or a trip to Barbados or a new designer suit.

I've always been inclined to just believe whatever Daddy believes. After all, he's been pretty much the singular driving force in my life. So, I walked into that animal shelter with a serious look on my face, totally prepared to turn off my heart and see it as a business transaction. But from the very second my eyes landed on little Henry, his fur all matted and his big brown eyes blinking sadly at me through the metal bars of his crate, I was a goner. There was no convincing my heart to forget about him. I have never loved another living thing the way I love that ridiculous little dog. He's about seven years old and he's lived with seven different caretakers, so he's been through the wringer, but none of that hardship has made him any less sweet and trusting. I took him home on day one of volunteering there. I just couldn't resist. It's been six months and I'm still just as enamored with the little guy as I was that first moment when he jumped into my arms, trembling but licking my face.

The tears burn in my eyes and I bite down hard on my lip, nearly drawing blood. I can't give in. I can't let myself break down and cry.

Still, I can't stop worrying about Henry. Who will feed him? Who will play with him? Whose bed will he sleep in if I'm not there? I promised him I would never abandon him and now here I am, shoved into some damp underground hole, unable to be there for him. Then I remember with a sigh of relief that he's not alone. I let Cassandra take him home with her last night, as she told me she has a great idea for a little photoshoot for him Monday morning before school. Although, as it occurs to me now, it's Monday today.

Which is great news for Cassandra and Henry.

I'm sure they're having a blast with their little photo-shoot. But for me, it's bad news. Because I don't have any classes on Monday. I don't even have volunteer hours scheduled. I generally just spend my Mondays on campus in the library, studying and poring over research for hours on end until I start to go cross-eyed and have to call it a night. That means I'm usually un-accounted for on Mondays. Nobody to look after me. No role call to count me in or out.

It means that nobody will even know that I'm missing until at least Tuesday. Cassandra is due to return Henry to me on Tuesday evening when she comes over to my place for her bi-weekly tutoring session. I already miss them both terribly, especially Henry, since he's been my constant sidekick and companion for six months. No creature or human on the planet has ever been so good at calming me down and brightening my lonely days than he has.

Sometimes I just look at Henry and wonder how I ever managed to survive so many years without him around.

I wish he was here right now. I would give anything to feel his soft, scruffy head resting on my knee, those big, expressive eyes peering up at me with adoration.

Again, I bite back the tears.

I don't know how long I have already been in this place. Could be hours. Could be all day. I also have no idea whether someone is going to come in and check on me anytime soon. I never even got to see my captor's face. By now, I have managed to wiggle my nose and twist my head back and forth just enough to loosen the blindfold around my eyes. Of course, it's completely pitch black in here, so it doesn't do me much good, but I sure wish I had gotten a chance to see who put me here.

He must be some kind of monster. A predator with a cruel face and a behemoth body. I wrack my brain, trying to drum up what all I do still remember about him. I can recall his brute strength more than anything. The way his powerful arms slid around me and so easily kept me bound to his muscular, broad chest. I can remember the sensation of large, calloused hands— the hands of a laborer or an artisan of some kind— running down my arms to bind my hands together. They're still tied even now, which is annoying because of the cramps in my wrists, but also because you never realize just how often you need to scratch an itch until you can't. I can't help but wonder if that's part of the torture. Another little detail intended to drive me insane and make me plead for mercy.

That only makes me feel more defiant, though. Because even though I have spent my whole life trying to be as obedient and exceptional as possible in a desperate bid for my distant father's approval, there's still that crackling ember of a flame inside me. It's a fire that has been steadily burning every day of my life, just enough to keep me propelled forward rather than shrinking back from the overwhelming challenges of my everyday life. That fire sustains me even as I try to please the one man nobody could ever please.

"Ugh," I groan. "Cassandra, I wish you were here."

I immediately feel kind of stupid for talking out loud to myself, but honestly, it's not as if there's anyone around to hear me anyway. I could sit here and sing the national anthem for hours on end and no one would know. I close my eyes and pull in a deep, slow breath, attempting to channel Cassandra's ability to dissect a situation. She's always been better at that than I am, despite the fact that I'm the math-minded one and she's the artist.

She has a flair for creativity, for seeing the threads that wrap around each life. If I toss a rock in the river, I can count the rings and the circumference and how far out they'll go, but she can see something broader, the space between the ripples. The impact the stone will have on the rest of the lake, not just on how it makes the water move.

But I just don't think of things the same way she does. All I can focus on is the ache in my wrists and the clammy smell clinging to my nose. I blink my eyes again and again, trying to find some shapes in the heavy darkness. I keep thinking that eventually my eyes will adjust to the lack of light, but—

My heart stops for a moment, my eyes going wide.

There's a soft, barely-audible sound on the other side of the door. At first I wonder if I'm just imagining it, but then I hear it again. Something akin to footsteps, muffled by dewy grass. A moment later, there's a tiny rectangle of light several feet in front of me. I realize slowly that it's a slot in the door, the soft light of late afternoon sunshine filtering through. But then something else swims into focus: within that rectangle of light I can make out two smallish, shining dark orbs. They blink and I gasp in fear, trying to wriggle backwards away from it.

Eyes. A pair of dark, penetrating eyes. Looking right at me.

"Wh-who are you?" I manage to cry out. My voice is hoarse, the fear clearly evident in the way it trembles. I hate it. I wish I could sound braver.

At first, the man is silent, just watching me with those deep, dark eyes. They're brown, but so dark as to nearly be black. I wish I could see more of his face, but at the same time… his eyes alone are frightening enough.

"Say something! Come on!" I hiss angrily.

More silence. I slump back against the earthy wall.

Then, finally, he speaks in a low, gruff voice. "You've removed your blindfold," he points out flatly.

"What else am I supposed to do in here?" I shoot back.

I hear what could possibly be a chuckle, but those black eyes don't waver for a second. I wait for him to say something else, but apparently, he's content just to watch me.

My stomach churns and uneasiness grips me. I don't like this. It feels wrong.

Even wronger than being kidnapped and held captive in the first place.

His stare somehow feels more intimate. More dangerous. More… threatening. I have to collect more puzzle pieces if I'm going to figure out how to escape.

"So, are you going to tell me who you are? Or why the hell you brought me here?" I ask, rather startled by my own defiance. He seems a little surprised, too, but also amused.

"You're very talkative for a captive," he notes.

"And you're very quiet for a kidnapper," I retort. "Are you going to hurt me?"

"That depends," he replies, sending a shiver down my spine.

"What? What the hell does that mean?" I ask, my voice muted with fear.

"If you will obey, you will survive," my captor responds matter-of-factly. "You have to be a good girl for me. Can you do that?"

I stare at his eyes, totally stunned by the demand.

On the one hand, I'm completely offended and indignant— he's speaking to me as though I'm a child. But on the other hand, there's something strangely exhilarating about what he's asked of me. Normally, I don't much enjoy being told what to do, but I must be losing my mind because it feels... different this time.

"I-I'll do my best," I reply, trying to appeal to him.

"If you're a good girl, if you behave, you will be rewarded," he states.

"I can do that," I insist desperately, scooting closer. "I promise. I'll be good."

"Yes," he grunted, "you will."

And with that, the little rectangle of light closed off and the eyes disappeared, leaving me lost and confused in the dark yet again. "Wait! No! Please, come back!" I cry out, but I can hear his soft footsteps getting quieter as he walks away.

LILA

"**G**et your grimy hands off of me!" I scream.

Dust kicks up under my feet as I spin around, yanking my oversized messenger bag down from my shoulder. I turn to face one of my attackers, an almost beastly snarl on my face as I glare at him. It frustrates me to no end that he's wearing a ski mask— they all are for some reason— because I want to see his face. I want to know exactly what this man looks like so I can have a before and after in my mind once I beat his face in with my bag. I have never been so grateful for the overly ambitious load of classes in my university schedule as I am right now, because my messenger bag is stuffed full of heavy textbooks, notebooks packed with intricate notes, and a bulging case of pens and pencils. The bag must weigh at least fifteen pounds, more than my little dog, Henry.

As soon as his precious, sweet little face pops into my

27

mind, I'm filled with a renewed sense of vengeance. These fuckers think they are going to capture me and take me away from Henry. They think they can just show up in my busy, tightly-wound microcosm of a world and shake it all up so easily, like I'm made of papier-mache. Like I'm some wimpy little waif just waiting to be scooped up and stowed away in a castle.

I'm no princess. I'm no damsel. Nobody is going to Rapunzel me.

There are three of them and one of me, but all of my attackers are regarding me more like a wild animal with rabies than a slender, petite co-ed. That's good. I want them to fear me. I want to keep them on their toes.

"Go on! Do your worst!" I hurl at them, spitting on the ground with rage. "Just try and take me, you filthy cowards! You have no idea who you're messing with."

"Calm down," one of them hisses, glancing around furtively.

It's still dark here on campus, the sun just starting to crown over the horizon. The sky is still that anemic shade of pale gray, the light barely illuminating the fluffy clouds above. Every tree and bush is shrouded in darkness, a hulking, mysterious shadow in the low light. The thought occurs to me that time is on my side. If I can just keep these guys at a safe enough distance for long enough, people will start showing up on campus. Students will start rolling in, half-asleep and bleary-eyed, for their early morning math classes. Professors will march across the grassy paths to their offices to prepare for a long day of teaching. The custodial staff will turn up to keep things clean and gleaming. After all, this is the Massachusetts Institute of Technology. This is an important place, filled with important, brilliant people. Overachievers like me who show up before the sun rises and don't leave until after the sun disappears back over the horizon. Surely, sometime soon, backup will get here and I'll be saved.

In the meantime, though, I have to fight.

All three of my masked assailants have their hands up, their tall, muscular frames carefully circling me as I wield my heavy messenger bag like a flail. I feel strangely powerful. Adrenaline pumps through my veins, but my heart is beating calmly and evenly. I never miss a beat. I never falter for even a moment. I am in total control here.

Finally, one of the masked men takes a dive toward me, but I'm prepared for him. With a throaty growl, I swing my bag at him and hit him hard in the shoulder. He cries out in agony, stumbling clumsily to the ground. His cohorts are so stunned by my attack that they hesitate— and their failure is my victory. I can clearly see the window of opportunity, and I take it.

I drop my bag and bolt in the opposite direction, the keys to my BMW roadster jangling reassuringly in my pocket. I'm running as fast as I can, breathing hard, never daring to look back. There is no need. I smile to myself, knowing that safety is just a few bounds away. I press the unlock button on my key fob over and over again as I run up to the driver's side door. I fling it open and slide behind the wheel, my hands trembling slightly as I jab the key into the ignition and give it a violent turn. But to my horror, I turn it too hard— and the key snaps in half.

I cry out, my eyes wide as I gaze at the shattered key in my palm. A moment later, the windshield shatters with an ear-splitting crack, and as the shards of glass pierce my face, I am jolted awake.

My eyes round and wide open, I sit there slumped against the muddy wall, my chest heaving as I gasp for breath. I look around myself, my heart sinking as reality comes trickling back in. I'm not on campus in my car. I didn't defend myself against my attacker.

He won the battle.

He captured me, and now I'm still sitting in this disgusting, dank hole waiting for him to carry out whatever sick punishment he has in mind for me.

I sigh and let my head fall back against the filthy wall behind me. I can feel the damp earth soaking through my hair to my scalp, and normally that would gross me out beyond belief. But right now, it doesn't matter. Nothing really matters, to be honest. Might as well get used to feeling gross and uncomfortable, because it seems as though my captor has no intentions of letting me go free anytime soon.

I only wish I knew how long I've been in here. Long enough to drift off into a dream, at the very least. I try to shift around, stretching out my legs with a groan of pain. It hurts. My whole body feels like one gigantic cramp at this point. I need to get up and move around. I would kill for the opportunity to do some simple yoga poses— anything to change positions and work out the kinks in my muscles. I have a strong feeling my captor isn't concerned with muscle tension on my part, however.

In fact, for all I know, he could be leaving me in here to waste away.

I shiver.

That's an even worse fate than dying in some contested battle. At least if I had to physically fight him, I could go down swinging. That's how I want to go. With a battle cry, not with a whimper. But that's not up to me anymore. I, Lila Hawthorne, girl who is continually in control of her own fate, can't do a damn thing to save herself from a slow, boring descent into madness or death.

"Yikes," I murmur to myself, shaking my head. "That's a little grim."

I force myself to think of it differently. My father would be so disappointed to see me give up so easily. Sure, he's always taught me to obey his commands and advice, but he's also always told me that I have to fight for myself. That I can't trust a man to look after me. They all want the same thing: to break me down and stamp out my spirit.

I summon up as much defiance and indignation as I can muster, focusing my anger toward my captor rather than at myself.

I wish I knew what time it is. My wrists are

bound behind me, so I suppose it wouldn't matter whether I'd worn that watch Daddy got for me or not. Besides, the guy who brought me here took all of my belongings: my purse, my messenger bag, my phone. He would have taken my watch along with the rest anyway. For a moment, I feel a glimmer of hope: maybe someone will have already realized I'm missing and will be tracking the location of my cell phone. That happens all the time in TV shows.

But then I remember with a sinking heart that my phone does not even possess that capability. Even though my father is very well-off and he could easily afford to give me an updated, fancy smartphone, he always insists that I'm too reliant on newfangled technology and that I need to do things the old-fashioned way. Everything my father has ever taught me has been in pursuit of creating a strong, battle-ready, but obedient daughter. He says today's technology has made me too soft, that I need to pull back a little and do things the way he does it. When I go to class, I'm the only student in the room who still takes notes exclusively in paper notebooks. All of my classmates use laptops and tablets or even just their phones. And their textbooks all exist in e-reader format, giving them a much lighter load to carry to and from class each day. But not me. I still use heavy, hardback textbooks, even when my professor urges me to do otherwise.

At the end of the day, I only answer to one man: my father.

It means that I'm always behind, always doing the analog way of things. Daddy wants me to work hard, and sometimes that means shoveling out far more effort than anyone else does.

So I have a flip-phone, one of those old ones that can't even access the internet. The GPS tracker is deactivated, and besides, it probably would not have worked very accurately anyway. Yes, it's the 21st century, but if Daddy says I have to do it the old way, then I'll do it the old way.

Of course, that doesn't help me one bit right now. Nobody is tracking my phone. They couldn't even if they wanted to. It's always been a point of pride for me: that I'm old-fashioned. I'm classic. I don't need those new technological advances to be an exceptional student or a phenomenal success of a daughter. I've always proven the naysayers wrong. I've always worked that much harder, poured that much more of my heart and soul into my work to balance it out and come out on top. Daddy won't raise a quitter, and he sure as hell won't raise a failure.

I could kick myself for letting him talk me into using one of those old flip-phone bricks. It would be so easy for someone to just flip on the GPS tracker and have them come find me if only…

"No. Don't think that way. There's no point," I scold myself out loud. "No use agonizing over what could have been. Come on. You can't go back in time. All you have is the present."

I'm wide awake. Might as well do as much research as I can while I'm conscious.

I start looking around, squinting in the almost perfect darkness of my holding cell. I can't move very easily, since my hands are still bound behind me, but I can lean from side to side a little. I frown, thinking that I might possibly be able to make out some strange markings on the wall to my left. Summoning up all the strength I can get, I lurch over toward the markings with a grunt. I nearly topple over in the process, but I manage to get close enough to follow the pattern of the marks. My stomach twists uncomfortably when I realize what I'm looking at.

Tally marks. A lot of them. Clearly meant to number a count of days stuck here. And they're not made in chalk or pen or pencil… they're obviously claw marks. Someone whittled the shit out of their nails to make these tally marks.

"Well, that's not great," I mumble, feeling sick to my stomach. I can't help but wonder what dark fate befell the person who was held here before me. How many have there been? How did they get here? How did they get out?

Why?

Suddenly, I feel a frantic need to busy myself. I have to get out somehow. I know I can't get through that door, so I just start scratching away at the dirty floor beneath me. I kick back dirt with the heels of my boots, digging and digging in the desperate hope of finding some secret door or something. But instead, I find something much worse: concrete. Underneath the layers of grime and filth is a cement floor, hard as rock and totally impenetrable. Again, tears burn in my eyes as hopelessness sets in.

But no sooner do I start to cry than I'm distracted by a strange new sound. A scraping noise that makes me swallow my sobs and I go silent with fear. I stare toward the door, totally paralyzed. For a moment I worry that madness is starting to sink in and I just imagined it, but then the door slowly creaks open. Soft evening moonlight falls like a pillar in front of me, illuminating an absolutely hulking dark silhouette. My captor. My lips open to cry out to him but no sound comes out. The next thing I know, I'm bowled over by the delicious, stomach-rumbling fragrance of hot soup and warm bread. I realize instantly how very hungry I am, and I hastily scoot forward, following the smell. I can see a small bowl and a tiny plate with a hunk of bread beside it, and my mouth waters. I manage to drag myself closer and closer to it before remembering that my hands are still bound behind my back.

I can't eat.

A moan of disappointment rolls from my throat and I glare up at the dark figure in front of me, blinking and trying to bring his face into focus. But he's blocking the light in such a way that it's difficult to make out his features. All I can tell is that he isn't smiling.

"This is bullshit," I murmur, shaking my head as I stare up at him. "You did this just to screw with me. You know damn well my hands are tied."

"Have you been good?" he asked, his voice deep and composed.

I frown, tilting my head to one side. "Yes. Of course, I have. I can't do anything else," I tell him, trying to hold back my rage. Clearly, that's not going to get me anywhere with him. I wait, my chest heaving, as he seems to size me up. Then, without warning, he starts moving toward me. Panic floods through my veins and my heart pounds, my breath coming in short gasps of terror. The man quickly bends down beside me. I'm so frightened that I don't even dare to steal a glance at his face in the light. I close my eyes tightly and brace myself for some kind of punishment. But to my infinite relief and shock, he doesn't hurt me at all. He reaches behind me and deftly unbinds my hands, then steps back into the doorway to look down at me.

I immediately start rubbing my wrists, wincing at the bruises left there but the cords. I can hardly believe it. I gaze up at him warily, wondering what I did to deserve that.

"I don't understand," I admit.

"You behave, you are rewarded," he answers simply. "Eat."

I look down at the soup and bread, unable to deny the growling in my stomach. I want to eat it. Desperately. But there's a part of me that worries it might be poisoned. Or that maybe it's a trick of some kind.

Besides, I still feel that fire of defiance. I don't want to do as I'm told.

"Eat," my captor repeats gruffly, a little louder this time.

"And what if I don't?" I ask, glancing up at him with my held head high.

"Then you'll be hungry."

It's such an easy, straightforward answer that I almost start laughing, but then I quickly resist the urge. "Why should I do what you tell me to do?" I press him, fully aware that I'm playing with fire but somehow unable to stop myself.

"I think I've made myself pretty clear, Lila," he says, and the way my name sounds on his lips makes me shiver in a way that confuses me. "Do what you're told, and you will be rewarded. It's really that simple. Eat."

This time, I don't know if it's because of the way he said my name or maybe just because I am, in fact, very hungry, I give in. I do as I'm told. I pick up the spoon and start to ravenously slurp the soup, taking nibbles of the bread in between sips. I can't help but groan a little in satisfaction. The food is surprisingly delicious considering the fact that I'm essentially eating it off of a dirt floor. And all the while, those dark eyes are locked on me, never blinking, never turning away for a second. When I hurriedly finish my food, I push the empty bowl, plate, and spoon back toward him and I scoot back a little, waiting for… something. I don't know what.

But when it happens, I realize what I'm waiting for.

He kneels down, still masked in darkness, and reaches out to touch my cheek. I freeze up, unable to pull away as his rough fingertips caress the side of my face. I don't know why, I can't even begin to explain it, but for some reason I lean into his touch hungrily. Desperately. He strokes my cheek once, cooing.

"Good girl," he whispers. "Very good."

I close my eyes, losing myself to the bizarre comfort of his warm hand against my face. I never want him to stop. I need him to stay close, even though there's a voice in the back of my head screaming, begging me to pull back, to not let him touch me. When he withdraws, I open my eyes and actually whimper, disappointed to lose his touch.

Silently, he takes something out of his jacket and slides it across the floor to me. I blink, squinting in the darkness to figure out what it is. I realize with confusion that it's a notebook of some kind, and there's a pencil poked through the spiral binding.

"What is this for?" I ask.

"To write in," my captor says directly. He stands up and I gulp, noticing once again how enormously tall and broad-shouldered he is. "You will be watched. Do not do anything to hurt yourself, Lila. I would hate to see you hurt."

I'm speechless, just staring at the notebook open-mouthed. But that's not the only gift he has for me. The next thing I know, he's handing me a neatly-folded bundle of clothing, and I realize with a sinking feeling that I recognize these clothes.

They're from my own closet. At home. Somehow, this man has been in my home. It hits me hard just how dangerous and unpredictable he is, that I'm standing so close to the flames. I should fear him.

I do fear him.

And yet, there is something about him that comforts me. It doesn't make any sense, but I decide to push it a little further. After all, who knows how long he will wait before coming back to visit me again?

"Please," I beg him, "I have a dog. He's a rescue. You have to let me talk to my friend— she's got my dog right now and she needs to know that I-I'm okay. Please."

There's a pause. Then he says, in the same even, controlled tone, "I can make no promises. But as long as everyone is as obedient as you have been tonight, then no one will be hurt. You could be out of here sooner than you think."

I'm stunned by his words, and it takes me a few seconds to process the meaning of them. By the time I'm ready to reply, he's already closing the door. My heart starts to pound as the darkness falls in around me once again.

"Please! Don't go! Come back! Don't leave me here alone," I cry out, crawling toward the door as it closes in my face.

LILA

*I*s this what it feels like in solitary confinement?

I sit here in the shadowy darkness, staring at the wall. My eyes roll across the faint scratchings in the earthy material, the vertical claw marks tallying up a daunting number of days and nights. The sight of them, the sheer number of lines etched into the wall, make me dizzy to look at them. The lines run together. I lose count. My mind won't let me approach the reality of what the previous tenant of this cell had to go through.

I know if I even begin to turn down that road, there's no telling what horrors my imagination will summon up from the depths of my fear and anxiety. It's like watching a horror movie alone in the dark. It always seems much scarier when the monster is still kept hidden, because the human mind is a peculiar and vividly-colored machine. Once the devil is revealed, he tends to lose some of his mystique, some of his inherent monstrosity. The viewer can then more easily categorize and therefore rationalize the monster. He's not as scary anymore after that.

I'm being held for ransom.

The conversation with my ransom spins around in my mind, over and over, but that's one thing I know for certain. *Everyone* has to behave. Not just me. I don't know if it was a slip up or if he simply wanted to let me know why I was kidnapped, but there's the simple, awful truth.

Sitting here, waiting as the minutes slide away slowly as molasses but much less sweet, I am tempted to believe that nothing could ever be so terrible as what my mind can think up. But I have an ache in my gut that warns me that truth is almost always stranger than fiction, and uglier, too. And those tally marks aren't just part of the austere decor of whatever this cell is supposed to be. They are real. Left here by a real human who used her real fingernails to scratch out the final days of her sanity, maybe even her life.

Maybe it's unfair for me to assume the person who was here before me was also a young woman. If my captors are operating under the assumption of a ransom deal, there's no way to really pin down what demographic are most likely to be held for that reason.

At least, it's not something I have ever stumbled across the data for. Surely it's out there, but that kind of thing has never mattered to me, not in my world. There's little space left for superfluous research or hobbies. I try to keep myself as busy and productive as possible.

My father has no tolerance for laziness, and he instilled in me a driving need to push further and climb the ladder. That's why I've been working to get my business degree. Business is one of the few concentrations my father deems worthy. It's easy to see why: he's a businessman himself, and a successful one at that. He never coddled me, even when I was a little girl. Daddy has made it abundantly clear that he will not accept weakness. He will not tolerate vulnerability. And he sure as hell will not allow frivolity.

Not until I've got my degree and have struck it rich in my own right. Then, he says, I can spend my hard-earned money however I see fit.

Still, there will be parameters then, too. Fancy cars. Designer clothing. Sprawling palatial winter home estates in Florida, opulent historic brownstone penthouses for summers in New England. Maybe even some couture handbags and clutches. Those are the expected symbols of luxury and success my father will allow me to buy when, someday, I follow in his enormous footsteps and make my way in the business world. That is all I live for:

mastering university so that I can use it as a stepping stone to the next realm I must conquer.

He will expect nothing short of perfection. I always intended to give that to him. But now I'm in stagnant waters.

I do not like to waste time. If I'm not in class, I'm studying for that class. If I'm not shadowing my father at work, I'm keeping notes and planning ahead for some distant future in his line of work. If I'm not volunteering at the shelter, I'm tutoring Cassandra in math. My only methods of winding down and relaxing, so to speak, are either cuddling with my little dog Henry, or shooting photos and videos with Cassandra for fun.

At night, I barely sleep. I try to get at least four hours a night, because years ago I read an article my father recommended to me that suggested four hours is the very least a successful human requires. If I sleep less, he instructed me, then I will have more time to be productive, but no less than four. Late to bed, early to rise. Be the last to clock out and the first to clock in.

Always productive. Always busy.

So having to sit here doing nothing but twiddling my thumbs and waiting for… an end that may never come is possibly the worst fate I can imagine. I've tried to keep myself entertained or at the very least, distracted. The dark-eyed man gave me a journal and a pencil, and I've been absentmindedly scribbling away in it despite the fact that I can hardly see through the darkness. Who knows what these pictures would look like in the light? Probably nonsensical. Lines unmatching with lines. Curves refusing to connect together. It's frustrating. Even the words I write probably aren't legible. I hate it— the feeling of failure and being out of control.

And then there's the loneliness. That many-horned beast that creeps up behind me and rests its hoary head on my shoulder, breathing putrid breath on my neck, making me shiver with dread. I don't want to be alone.

It makes me sick to think about, but there's a gnawing sense growing in me that I am desperate for my captor to return. Even if it's just to taunt me or even hurt me, I want him to come back. I need to hear his low, growling voice. I long to feel his calloused hands running over my smooth skin. I want his ultimatums and his demands and his everything.

"What is the matter with me?" I whisper aloud, horrified by my own desires.

I should hate him. I should want him to stay as far away from me as humanly possible. But I don't hate him. I am confused by him, even intrigued, but I still want him to return. More than anything. Maybe even more than freedom.

I know how messed up that sounds. Perhaps it's just Stockholm Syndrome. Maybe I'm just losing my mind. Whatever the reason, there's only one solution: to be near him again.

Almost as though I've summoned him here with my thoughts, I jerk away in surprise when I hear the metal door start to slide open again. My heart begins to pound fiercely in my chest, making me gasp for air as I stumble back, eyes wide and expectant. I wait as the door slowly, agonizingly scrapes open. It's still dark outside, but there's a faint, eerie glow that suggests the uncanny hours during which the moonlight fades into the first early shimmers of sunrise. I imagine it must be sometime between midnight and four in the morning.

The witching hour, my thoughts remind me.

Has the handsomest version of the devil yet come to see me again?

I very nearly lick my lips in anticipation, hastily fumbling to stand up. My chest is heaving, my whole body aching and twinging and tingling for him. I need to hear his voice. I need him to tell me what to do.

I need a task, something to focus on. I can't handle this boredom anymore.

At first, I see the same thing I saw before: the dark, tall silhouette of a powerful man standing in the glowy light of the doorway. He looms over me, just like before, his physical prowess dwarfing me and making me feel insignificant. Like a sparrow trembling before a wolf.

He takes a long stride forward and I lurch back, my arms reaching out to brace myself against the filthy wall behind me. I can hardly remember to breathe as he watches me. But then something, some bare animal instinct rolls down my spine. I freeze up, noticing that a detail that is somehow… off.

I remember so vividly that my captor's eyes are dark. So dark as to be nearly black. But this man in front of me now has lighter-colored eyes. A shade of pale green. It's a different man altogether. A terrible thought occurs to me: do I have more than just the one captor?

The green eyes blink and I sense a smile pulling at the corners of this strange new man's lips as he surveys me hungrily. I feel like a cornered animal, shrinking myself down as small and non-confrontational as possible. I don't want to invoke some kind of rage or defense in him. I just want him to leave me alone.

The other man made himself clear. If I behave, I won't get hurt. If I'm a good girl, I'll get rewarded.

This man is a complete enigma, and that's terrifying. There's no rule book for how to deal with him, and I'm knocked off balance by the realization that it's not just a single man keeping me locked up. It hadn't even occurred to me that I would be outnumbered, and the thought knocks the wind from my chest.

I have spent these long, empty hours building my

captor up in my mind, creating a fantasy image of the black-eyed man to comfort me in the shadows and silence. A dark anti-hero, perhaps. A villain with a code, someone who doesn't want to hurt me, but needs me as a bargaining chip to get what he wants.

But now he's just a member of a group. I pray it's only the two.

The green-eyed man takes another step closer through the threshold and I press myself to the back wall, desperate to keep as much space between us as I can. He continues to stare at me, and I can hear the faint, rasping drag of his breaths in and out, slowly.

Finally, I find my voice and push it into the air.

"What—what do you want? Who are you?" I ask, wincing at how my voice trembles and shakes, the fear so clearly evident in my tone.

The green-eyed man chuckles, but there is no mirth to the sound. It's pure evil, pure cruelty. He's laughing at me. He knows he's in control. But he doesn't say a word. He just stands there, looming over me like some behemoth, like a predator toying with his vulnerable prey. I have no way to fight back against him.

"Are you going to say anything? Or just stand there like a creep?" I accuse.

He says nothing but I see him shift his weight from one foot to the other, his enormous hands curling into tight fists at his sides. I swallow hard, realizing I might have pushed him too far. It only gets worse when he reaches back and pulls the door shut, leaving us both in the dark together. I can hardly even make out his gigantic shape in front of me. I start to hyperventilate, my legs quaking beneath me as he slowly takes a lumbering step closer to me. I push myself into the wall as hard as I can, turning my head to one side and grimacing. I don't dare close my eyes, trying to watch him approach even though my vision is almost totally darkened.

He's coming for me. And I have no defense against him.

Oh god. What have I done?

But then I hear the door creak open again. Confused, I glare around the green-eyed man just in time to see another dark figure come rushing through the door. I let out a scream of terror, watching as the second man tackles the first man to the filthy floor. I stumble away into a corner, my hands clasped over my mouth.

The second man wrenches the green-eyed man's arms behind his back, both of them grunting and scuffling against each other. But the second man is clearly the stronger one, and he manages to slam green-eyes into the metal door with a loud CLANG! I gasp, sinking down to the floor and throwing my arms up over my head instinctively. I watch through a gap in my fingers as the green-eyed man struggles to break free from the man holding him pinned against the door.

"Let me go," he hisses, desperately wriggling in the other man's grasp. He reminds me oddly of a fish on a hook, flopping around. But the man holding him there doesn't even seem to be breaking a sweat. This is all too easy for him.

"You have to learn your place," snarls my captor. I recognize him this time for certain: it's the dark-eyed man from before. My heart races wildly.

"Oh, and I suppose you think you're going to be the one to teach me?" rebukes the green-eyed man. His insolence is rewarded with a swift kick to the backs of his knees. He bellows out in pain, doubling over and barely holding himself up. By now, I'm using all of my self-control on trying not to scream. I don't want that power and rage to turn on me.

"I'd watch that lip if I were you," warns the dark-eyed man coolly. "You know you're not allowed down here. This isn't part of your job description. Lila is mine. You'll do well to remember that."

A little thrill of mingled horror and delight runs down my spine. Goosebumps prickle up on my skin as I listen to my captor defend me. Claim me. I feel a strange, foreign sensation taking hold of me. A deliciously wrong sort of tingling between my thighs.

Again, I wonder what the hell is wrong with me.

Dark-eyes tosses me a quick glance, a piercing gaze that lasts only a moment but which shakes me down to my very core. I hold my breath, eyes wide as his cherished attention is directed toward me just for a second. Then he yanks the green-eyed man through the doorway, roughing him up in the process. I can't help but revel in the intense adrenaline pumping through my veins, the exhilaration of watching my captor defend my honor, call me his own. I'm so disappointed when the door closes that I actually let out a little whimper. I go rushing to the door, pressing my ear against the cold metal to try and eavesdrop.

A moment later, there's a click as the little slot opens. To my surprise, my captor is at the slot, and for a split second I get to feel his hot breath tickle my cheek. I yelp and fall back, all the hairs on the back of my neck standing up. Those black eyes are watching me, unblinking. Unabashedly. He watches me like I'm something fascinating, something truly precious. I step up to the door, wanting— needing— to be closer to him.

The door locks with a resounding click, and I can faintly hear the clunky footsteps of the green-eyed man slinking away. The fear in my body starts to wane, only to be replaced by shimmering, undeniable desire.

"I apologize," my captor says smoothly. "My associate is a pig."

"But you saved me," I whisper back. I lift one trembling hand and cautiously poke my fingertips through the slot. I bite my lip, waiting for his response. Finally, he raises a hand and presses his calloused fingertips against mine, sending shockwaves of joy through my frame.

"Things are taking longer than they should," he tells me, with a hint of something like sadness. "I'm sorry. This should have ended by now."

"What should've ended? What is going on? Please, just tell me. I-I'll do anything to help. I promise I won't run away. I won't tell anyone," I ramble, shaking my head so fervently that my long hair swishes over my shoulders.

"You know I can't allow that, Lila," he replies softly. Again, his lips forming my name gives me a thrill that feels downright immoral. Still, my heart sinks at his reply.

"Okay. I guess that makes sense," I sigh. "But then… could you at least do me a favor, please? I just — I just want my school binder."

There's a pause, his fingertips frozen still against mine.

"Why?" he asks with some trepidation.

"Because it has photos of my dog slid under the lamination, okay? I just want to see my dog. It'll help me… feel less alone. I guess," I confess.

Again, a pause. Then, without a word, he pulls away and walks off, the slot sliding shut. Tears burn in my eyes and I blink them back angrily. Of course I've asked too much. Why the hell would my kidnapper let me have photos of my dog? He doesn't give a damn about me. I rest my forehead against the door for what feels like hours, but could easily be minutes. I don't know. It doesn't matter anyway.

Then, the slot opens back up, and I'm so surprised that I nearly stumble back onto my ass. But I manage to right myself just in time for a few items to be handed through: my binder, complete with cute pictures of Henry, and a small metal tray containing a cup of steaming, fragrant tea and a small hunk of bread similar to what I was given before.

"Take it," urges the dark-eyed man.

Remembering how to move, I reach out and obey, taking the tray and binder from him. I set the tray on the floor and clutch the binder to my chest, blowing gently on the hot tea as I stare through the slot in confusion.

"It's herbal tea," he says flatly. "Caffeine-free. I know it's not easy to sleep in there."

"It's not very comfortable," I agree. "But thank you."

I poke my fingers through the slot again. I get the same thrill when he touches his fingertips to mine. The loneliness in my heart aches far worse than the cramps in my body.

"What day is it now?" I ask softly. "Tuesday?"

"Yes. Tuesday night," he replies.

"This might be a strange question to ask you

but… is anyone looking for me yet? Does anybody know I'm missing?" I press him, worried that this might be a step too far.

But he simply answers, "There's been nothing on the news."

"Nothing," I repeat incredulously, sadness washing over me. "Nothing at all. But—but what about Cassandra? She'll notice I'm missing."

"That's already been taken care of," my captor explains. My stomach lurches.

"What? What does that mean? Did you hurt her? Oh my god," I gasp.

"No. Nothing like that," he assures me. "I've called you in sick to class for this week. Same goes for your volunteer gig. And your tutoring job."

"Oh," I murmur, unable to figure out if I'm more distressed or comforted by his intimate knowledge of my life.

"I don't know if it's good or bad that you know about all that," I muse aloud. "Even my own father doesn't know that much about my schedule."

I feel him stiffen up a little, his fingertips pressing gently against mine.

"Your father must be insane. If you were my daughter," he begins in a gruff voice, "I would be obsessed with you."

Suddenly, I feel an electric jolt roll through me. He pulls back his fingers almost as though he'd been electrocuted, and the slot clattered shut, nearly slicing the tips of my fingers as I snatched them back to my chest.

"Wait! Don't leave me alone," I cry out, tapping on the door.

"I will be watching your door tonight," my captor answers firmly.

"Come back," I murmur, laying my cheek against the closed slot. "Please."

"I'll be nearby," he promises, and then all goes quiet.

CHAINS

This one's different. There's something about her I can't put my finger on, and it isn't just her looks. I knew it from the moment I first held her in my arms. I could feel it in her. She's different, and I don't know if I like it or not.

But I'm a man of my word. That's why I'm leaning against the wall of the open-air hallway with my arms crossed, watching the cell door where yet another spoiled little rich girl is biding her time, waiting for her daddy to pay her ransom.

The hair on my arms prickles as I feel a chilly breeze in the November evening air. It turns out that my usual t-shirt and jeans isn't the most weather appropriate outfit for the Massachusetts autumn nights, but I've always been able to put up with the cold. Part of me likes it that way. It keeps me alert, always moving, never too relaxed. Besides, my thick beard keeps my face warm, and I've never needed much more.

The hallway is below ground but open to the outdoor sky, and it consists of a concrete walkway leading from one of the main buildings of this complex to the small root cellar where we have the girl stashed away safely.

Lila.

I've always thought of them as just "the girl," but this one's name keeps going through my head instead. She isn't the first, and she won't be the last. Not as long as there are more marks out there to make a payday out of.

That main building the sidewalk connects to isn't just any old abandoned building me and the guys moved into. It wasn't that long ago that this place was thriving with activity— and not the good kind. It used to be filled with the pained howling of patients, the grunting of inmates, and the sounds of runaway boys getting into fights.

I know, because when this place was operational, I spent a year here.

They put me here when my own dad died, and it took Mom a full year to get me out. Not even she could hold onto me, though. By that time, it felt like the world was just dead-set on keeping me from having a normal childhood, and it sure as hell didn't hold back on the punishment.

This place used to be a pretty complex on the

surface, I'd give it that. Some private company poured millions into this nightmare, probably wanting to make a quick buck off the prison labor they had us all doing. Inmates, mental patients, and runaways alike were all prisoners here, and it was part of what hardened me into the man I've become. I still remember my first night all too vividly, getting pulled out of my threadbare cot by the ankles and beaten by the other boys. They didn't let up until I knocked the front teeth out of their leader. There was nobody for me to turn to back then, nobody to look up to.

Didn't take long for me to realize there never would be.

It's funny. These days, now that the place has been long since abandoned, locals like to spread the rumor that the place is haunted. They say the mad spirits of the people who died here never found their way out. They say if you sneak in and aren't careful, there's a good chance you'll join them, getting dragged back to your own private slice of hell by ghostly nurses.

I'm not the kind of guy who believes in that kind of thing, but one thing's for sure: me and the rest of the gang chasing off teenagers who come snooping around every now and then sure helps the place's reputation.

Part of me is disappointed the old asylum has a worse reputation now than it used to. It's much more peaceful now, and I kind of like the way the creeping ivy looks as nature slowly starts to reclaim the rusty old bars and weathered brick.

The spirit of New England is a crumbling old asylum full of haunted memories.

My eyes are turned up toward the sky as the last of the sun's light goes away, starting to let twinkling stars show themselves one by one. I know the stars pretty well. Not many people know that. But having hours with nothing else to do gives you a lot of time to think, and over the years, I've gotten to know the map of the stars above me intimately.

It gives me time to think.

I hear a faint stirring from the root cellar, and my eyes flit down to the door for a moment. The girl moves around in there a lot. It's understandable. She's cold. The last few pieces of clothing I gave her should have been enough to keep her warm, but if her dad drags things out, I might have to get her something warmer. Maybe some thicker leggings and scarf, or a warm hat. She's a small slip of a girl.

Grabbing her was almost too easy.

This is nothing personal. It's how the guys and I make our living: ransom money. We track down bankers who've made their riches by foreclosing on people's houses, and we take the most precious thing they have from them— usually a spoiled, bratty daughter. Rich men love treating their daughters like prized possessions. Pretty trophies just like their cars and their yachts. Taking them always gets their attention.

It was my idea. I have no remorse. I have a special hatred in my heart saved up only for men like that.

After all, they're the sole reason I got dealt a sore hand in life— their greed. If it weren't for men like that, my dad might still be alive. My mom might still have a house. I might have…

I snap myself out of my trek down memory lane. I can feel the anger welling up in me like a storm. It happens every time I let myself think about everything that's happened to me over the years, all to line the pockets of some assholes who didn't even give a single mom and her scared kid a second thought after pocketing the profits. It gets my blood running hot and raring for a fight, and it has taken me a lifetime to get that side of me under control.

Rage is a powerful tool, but only if you can channel it. Otherwise, it destroys you, gleefully.

But I listen to the stirring of the dirt inside the makeshift cell, and I can't help wonder what my life would have turned out like if things had held together for me. I wonder if I'd be a clean-cut kind of guy. I wonder if I'd be the kind of guy who could draw in a girl like Lila and give her the type of life she deserves.

The kind of man she deserves.

I run my hand over my face, rolling my eyes at myself. Now I'm just fantasizing like a stupid kid.

There's no point in letting my thoughts go in that direction. Just because the leftover smell of her perfume is still on my jacket doesn't mean I should be letting her get to my head. It would be a rookie mistake. I have her here for one reason and one reason alone.

I'm no Prince Charming sweeping anyone off their feet. I'm a gang leader clapping a hand over their mouths and dragging them away to the shadows.

Just then, a sound reaches my ears, and I snap my attention to the left, back down the hall toward the building. As soon as I do, I feel all that rage boil to the surface again.

Ryder is standing there, his green eyes staring right back at me as he freezes in place. I didn't even hear the door of the building creak open. I hadn't told anyone that I was taking up guard duty for our hostage.

He was sneaking out here again.

"Hey!" I bark, and without waiting for a response, my whole body roars into motion.

Adrenaline surges through my body with nearly blinding anger as my massive frame barrels down the concrete, leather boots thumping hard against the ground as I race toward Ryder. In the split second that all takes place, his eyes widen, and he's frozen like a deer in the headlights for a second before he turns to try to run to the nearest wall. He jumps up on it, trying to get a hold on one of the stones to haul himself up and over the edge onto the grassy hill surrounding the open pathway.

I beat him to it.

My legs thrust me up, and I wrap my thick arms around his waist before he can pull himself away. Between the two of us, nearly four hundred pounds of man come crashing back down onto the sidewalk.

He grunts as he tries to pull himself away from me, but I have a hold on his jacket. He tries to struggle out of it, but I jerk it around, keeping him too disoriented to break free from me. He starts throwing wild swings up at me, and a few catch me on the arms, but there has never been any question about the pecking order in my gang.

I'm the top dog, and anyone who tries to question that gets punished.

Once I get my feet planted on the ground, I haul Ryder to his feet and immediately slam him back against the hard wall. I hear his head hit the back of the wall hard, and he lets out a grunt of pain. It's nothing compared to what I'm about to give him.

In the blink of an eye, I pull my fist back and swing. My punch catches him right in the center of the gut, and the sharp, pained wheeze I hear from his big chest tells me I've knocked the wind out of him.

He starts to slump to the ground, but I follow him down, never letting go of his jacket. He squints up at me, desperately trying to get his breath back as

I hold my fist just inches from his mouth and grit my teeth.

"That," I snarl, "was a lesson, Ryder."

Our eyes lock for a few moments, but his shuddering breaths can't give me an answer.

"Next time, it'll be a knife. I don't want to see your sorry ass past those doors anymore," I growl, pointing to the doors he came through from the main building. "Now get the fuck out of my sight."

I let him go and stand up in the same motion, taking a few steps back. Immediately, Ryder staggers to his feet and hurries down the sidewalk back through the doors, coughing and spluttering as he goes. I glare after him, still feeling the urge to kill coursing through me, barely held back by the restraint I've trained myself to use over the years.

My gang and I are close, but that doesn't mean I don't have to keep them in line every now and then. And with Ryder, I have to do it more often than I'd like, as much as I hate having to beat the shit out of my high school best friend to keep him in line. I thought about putting Bear on guard duty for this girl, since this kind of thing wouldn't be a problem with him, but I don't fully trust anyone but myself with her.

Nobody else can keep her safe like I can.

I hear the sound of tapping on metal, and I look over my shoulder. It's coming from the cell. Lila is knocking.

I take slow, careful steps toward the door, breathing slowly as I go. I want to get my blood settled down a little before I talk to her. She's scared enough of me as it is. It's better that way, of course, but I don't want her to be in a panic the whole time she's here.

My heavy footsteps bring me to a halt outside her door. The tapping stopped a few seconds ago. She must be able to tell how close I am.

"Hello?" her muffled voice calls. "What was that noise? Is…is everything okay?"

My jaw tightens. I sense the question behind her words is whether that scuffle was the sound of her rescuers arriving to save the day. I almost feel bad for her, but there's no help like that on the way. I wasn't lying when I told her there was nothing in the news. Her dad no doubt cares too much about appearances to go to the media.

My hand flexes as she waits for a reply. I have to resist opening the cell window. Lila is different in a way that I can't explain, and it makes me feel strange about her. Still, as the breeze blows over me again, I'm reminded that it's a cold night that'll be hard enough on her as it is. She might not sleep if she's worried something is going on outside, and that'll only make her condition worse.

Against my better judgment, I grip the metal handle and slide the food window open so I can peer through.

Her frightened face is surprisingly close to the door when I put my face close to it. I remember the pencil I gave her, and I don't push my eyes up against the window. I don't know if she's smart enough to try any bullshit like that, but I can't be too careful.

"It was nothing," I say curtly. "Don't worry about it."

I put my hand on the window to close it again, but her eyes go wide.

"Wait!"

I don't know why I listen to her. I've ignored that exact word so many times before slamming this very same window on all the other spoiled brats I've made a buck off.

"What?" I growl.

She moves her mouth, but no sound comes out. She seems as surprised as I am that she managed to keep my attention.

"D-don't close the slot!" she breathes, and I can hear the desperate edge in her voice.

"It's cold tonight," I say. "A draft will come in."

"I…" she started, grasping for words, terrified that I'll seal her away in darkness again so soon. "Please, can…can you leave it open tonight? I think-I think I'll sleep better if I know you're out there."

I glare in at her, searching those pleading blue eyes for her motives. This cell is secure, there's no way she could get out even with the window open. I can see all the way to where she sleeps from here if it's open. I just assume hostages would rather have privacy.

Whatever. If this girl has some weird, harmless requests, at least it'll make her more cooperative.

"Fine," I grunt, but I don't move away from the door.

A look of relief washes over her face, and a sincere smile crosses her features. After the rush of the fight with Ryder, her smile is strangely heart-warming to me.

"Thank- thank you," she stammers. "I… I appreciate it."

She looks like she wants to talk more, but she knows how little I speak by now. I do that on purpose. Getting too cozy with the hostage is a good way to let your guard down. After a few awkward moments, she bites her lip and moves back from the door, going to a pile of her old clothes she seems to have turned into a crude bedding area, and she lies down slowly.

She glances back at me one more time to make sure I'm watching, and it puzzles me that she seems genuinely comforted by knowing I'm watching her. I figure it's because of Ryder. Strange, but a cooperative hostage is better than a hostile one.

I can't shake the feeling that I'm acting like more of a protector than a captor at this point. I shouldn't have to play that part, but now that I'm doing it, I can't deny that it feels a little more rewarding than having to deal with some screaming and kicking little brat.

Once she gets as comfortable as she can, I take a few quiet steps back to the other side of the wall, and I lean against it again, crossing my arms and watching her small frame rise and fall with every breath. It's kind of relaxing to watch.

My phone buzzes and snaps me out of it. I take it out and read the text I just got from Bear, and my heart jumps.

The target's ready to negotiate.

The headlight beams in front of the car light up the flecks of drizzle falling in the midnight darkness. We roll around yet another forested curve on the seemingly endless road to the meeting point, and not a word passes in the car among the three of us.

I'm driving, and Ryder is in the passenger's seat. I don't want him out of my sight for a second. We're away from Lila, but I need to remind him that I have my eye on him. I need to keep him in my sight, at least out of the corner of my eye, until I feel like he's ready to fall back in line and not need to be watched as if I'm his babysitter.

Hawk and Tank went ahead of us much earlier. They've been staking the place out, making sure things are safe— that meant keeping an eye out for cops setting up a trap, if the mark was foolish enough to go to the police. Those two brothers joined up as a team, and they're fiercely loyal to each other. Not so much that I ever have to worry about them, though. They've been working with the rest of us for a long time, and I trust them as much as anyone else.

Bear is back at the asylum, keeping an eye on Lila.

I don't like the idea of leaving her alone, even if there's no chance of her getting out on her own, but Bear is the only one I can trust with her besides myself. He's a giant of a man with body hair so thick I swear it could make a knife glance off of him, and his love life is full of men, not women. That, and out of the lot of us, he's probably the softest soul deep down.

That's one thing I can't compete with— I was hardened long ago, and I don't think there would be any going back for me even if I wanted it.

Our vehicle swings around the final bend to our destination, and we turn off down a narrower road off to the side with crumbling asphalt all around it. The trees and shrubs are growing more free and wildly out here, slowly trying to take back the road and seal off our destination forever. People don't drive out to this place often, and that's exactly why we picked it for this ugly business.

Our headlights fall on the sign for the amusement park that's been shut down since the early nineties. Rust and chipping paint have almost eaten through the old ticket price and kitschy artwork on the sign. A few yards further down the road, it opens up into the long-abandoned parking lot, already sprouting tufts of weeds that have burst through the black asphalt in open rebellion.

We roll past it down a service road that leads to a small cul-de-sac surrounded by the trailers of what used to be part of a shabby amusement park. We bring the car to a halt while still in the woods, and my eyes scan the area warily.

"Think we have something to worry about from this guy?" Ryder asks.

"We have something to worry about from all of 'em," I say.

"Yeah, I meant more than usual," he says.

"Assume the worst," I say grimly. "Always. Guns loaded, eyes open. We've used this place before. You know what to look for."

They're the same words I say every time we prepare to get out of the car and make this deal happen. It would be repetitive, but careless mistake that could be avoided with a simple reminder are what make operations like ours fall apart all the time. We don't have to be geniuses. We just need to check the basics more than the other guys.

We climb out of the car, and we start making our way on foot around the cul-de-sac to the big trailer that used to be used as a kitchen— one of those overpriced restaurants where you get a deep-fried version of just about anything you could imagine that you'll regret later. Ryder walks a few paces to my right, and I sent them a text to let Hawk and Tank know we're close. They should be holed up in the ruins of what used to be a petting zoo by now. It's a good place to hide and watch, and it's eerie enough that not even the teenagers like going there often.

It's also a great place to use for an ambush, so I always have the brothers investigate it while Ryder and I handle the business. I do the talking, and he stands at my side for backup. All four of us would make the contact jumpy.

There are two other trailers and temporary buildings set up: a stage where magicians did tricks, and a funhouse that's really just an elaborate version of the kids' play areas they have in fast food restaurants. The place is caked in graffiti from the teenagers who've snuck up here from time to time to drink and break some bottles, but that hasn't done much to lift the haunted feeling from the derelict park.

We aren't supposed to be meeting a person tonight. If anyone else is here, we have a problem. The mark has instructions to leave the money for Lila's ransom in the last broken oven in the kitchen. Once we confirm that we have the money, we arrange to have the girl dropped off at a different location that we don't disclose until she's dropped off and we're long gone. It's efficient, safe, and usually clean. For these rich assholes, it's much safer and quieter to just pay the money rather than getting the police involved.

The parents want the girl back, and they have far, far more than enough money to make it happen quickly and easily. Getting the police involved means publicity, and that's bad for everyone involved.

I climb up into the sea of broken glass and rubble that used to be a restaurant, or what passed for it at one time. My boots crunch against the glass as I make my way through, glancing around cautiously. My hand is on my gun, and I'm ready to act quickly, but I don't take it out yet. There could be some teenager or a homeless person creeping around, and I wouldn't want to even run the risk of pointing the barrel at a person like that who didn't deserve it.

Besides, if there's a police trap set up here, our best bet is to split up and disappear into the woods before we can regroup. That's our plan, and it always has been. A firefight is not productive.

We take a few steps into the trailer, and I can see the oven from where I stand. The words *ORDER UP* are spray painted on the wall under the hole where fry cooks used to hand food to the serving staff, and there are a couple used needles lying on the floor just under that. Tables and chairs have long since either been carried off or the rusty ones left to decay. Everything looks just like we left it last time we were here.

…but something feels off.

I stop, and I look around with a furrowed brow as Ryder continues walking forward slowly, inspecting the place. We don't say a word to each other while we're on the job like this. Don't want to risk drawing attention to this neck of the woods for any reason.

As Ryder walks forward, he enters the kitchen, like I've seen him do plenty of times on his way to the oven. When he does, it hits me.

The lighting in here is different.

The full moon is just barely casting light through the scattered drizzling clouds, but it's enough for me to be able to tell that everything looks slightly different in the trailer-restaurant, and when Ryder reaches the oven and puts his hand on it, I notice what's different.

The window opposite where Ryder is standing has been shattered open. It used to be so caked in grime that it kept the room dark, so dark that rats would usually scurry away when we entered. I take a step into the kitchen and see that it has indeed been punched through…thoroughly.

As I furrow my brow, I feel my phone buzz, and I glance at it to see a text from Tank. He wouldn't message me unless it were urgent.

Someone's in the fun house

My eyes snap up, and I see that the window in the kitchen has a straight line of sight to the top level of the fun house.

"Get down!" I bark at Ryder as I barrel forward, and every muscle in my body kicks into gear as adrenaline lets me race forward toward him. He looks up and back at me just a split second before I reach him.

Our bodies make contact just as I hear the gunshot of the hunting rifle.

I feel a bullet fly so close to my head that I could have sworn it brushed against the hair on my neck. Ryder and I hit the ground with a heavy, painful thud as the bullet hits the wall behind the oven.

This is a fucking trap.

"What the fuck?!" Ryder shouts.

"Sniper in the funhouse!" I bark, and without a second thought, I take off running through the other end of the trailer.

The back end that used to be used by the staff has long since had its door torn off, and thick brush has already started creeping inside. I take a running dive into it, and I hit the ground rolling, feeling my skin get scratched by the twigs. I start barreling through the brush around the cul-de-sac, not willing to run out into open territory.

That would be a death sentence, but we have one

other thing working to our advantage— whoever is here must not know about Tank and Hawk.

I hear two gunshots go off from the old petting zoo, and I hear them ricochet off the funhouse. When the bullets hit, I see what they saw moving on the top level: a dark figure in one of the windows, right in front of the distortion mirrors. He slips back further inside when my men shoot at him, and that gives me the cover I need.

I dart out across the cul-de-sac, heavy boots hitting the ground hard as they propel me forward to my target. I reach the front of the funhouse in a matter of seconds, and in one fluid motion, I take hold of the rusty bars that used to form the queue, and I haul myself up and over into the entrance.

I take my gun out, holding it in front of me as I enter the house while I hear Tank and Ryder circling around the outside and back. I walk through a cylindrical hallway that used to turn slowly when the park was operational. There's very little room to hide here, and if the assassin is good, he'll take advantage of that.

I round the corner with my gun forward, and almost immediately, I see the glint of a knife as the attacker lunges forward. I fire my gun, but it hits the metal ceiling and makes the whole room ring as I twist away to avoid the knife.

The man is dressed in a similar set of dark clothes, turtleneck, and black beanie as my gang and

I are. He's also clearly no amateur. He wastes no time recovering from his missed attack, and I don't have time to aim my weapon before he comes at me again. He's brought a knife to a gunfight in one of the few possible situations where that would be a good idea.

I put a gloved hand around his forearm when he lunges forward, but I can't get the grip I need to twist the knife out of his hand, and I'm forced to drop my gun. Immediately, I kick it into the darkness so that he can't grab it either, but he doesn't seem interested in it.

I can feel the strength in his arms alone, and I know he thinks he doesn't need it.

If we were just some random gang of thugs, he might actually have the upper hand here, but I'm not going to let him have that.

We grapple. I try to get the knife from him while he tries to swing it around to drive the point into any part of me he can reach, but I can tell which parts he's going for— throat one moment, kidneys the next, then the gut. I narrowly avoid him, but when he tries to stab me in the gut, I twist away just late enough that the blade rips my shirt. The turtleneck is almost in shreds over my shoulders, but I don't have time to care.

His knife comes down so close to my face that I feel it brush against my beard, and I move in around his side, taking the one opportunity I see. With one hand, I get a grip on his wrist and tighten my fist until I hear a crunch on the downswing. The assassin lets out a howl of pain, and in the same motion, I drive my knee into the back of his.

It sends him to the ground on his knees, hard, and I waste no time in wrenching the knife from his grip and putting it to his throat.

The second I finish, Ryder staggers into the funhouse after me, gun out and ready, flashlight in another hand.

We lock eyes as I hold the attacker at knifepoint. We don't say a word. We don't need to.

Ryder knows every bit as well as I do that I just saved his life. He gives me a solemn nod, and I take it as a vow that he won't do so much as *think* out of line ever again. If he does, he's not the man I grew up with.

I hear the sounds of footsteps behind me, but I recognize the gaits— it's Tank and Hawk.

"Got a live one," I say gruffly once the whole gang is inside with me.

"Who is he?" Ryder asks, stepping forward.

"Answer," I order the assassin, pressing the knife to his throat.

"You know who sent me," the man says grimly. His voice is rueful, but he doesn't make a move to try to struggle away.

"You're a professional," I remark. "You were paid good for this, weren't you? I got questions."

"A shame," he growls, and I realize that he has been inching his hand closer to his belt while we spoke.

The second he grips the holster of the gun and pulls it out, I drop the knife, put my hands around his neck, and I give it one hard, firm twist.

The sound of his neck breaking echoes in the metal room, and the man's body slumps to the ground before I grab the gun in a gloved hand, looking around at the others with a set jaw.

"Let's move. We have a problem."

~

Back at the asylum a few hours later, fresh out of the vehicle, I throw the door to the walkway open and march down to where I see Bear standing guard outside the root cellar.

"Holy shit," he says when he sees me storming forward, turtleneck in rags and fire in my eyes. "What the fuck happened out there?"

"Good question," I say curtly. "Go inside. I need a word with her."

He stands back as I storm up to the heavy iron door, slide the key into the padlock, and pull it open, and see Lila sitting at the back of the room. Her face goes white as she sees me stride into the room in heavy, menacing steps, and I slam the door behind us.

I wake from a dark dream to find myself in an even darker reality. As soon as my eyes flutter open, I know what woke me up: the sound of the lock being disengaged and the metal door creaking open. It's still dark, that hazy glow faintly shining through and confusing my mind. It could be twilight, it could be dawn— I have no way of knowing. I remind myself that I should be trying to keep tabs on the days and nights.

Maybe I should be etching lines into the filthy, earthen wall like the tenant who came before me. Maybe that's the only way to cling to some tiny, thin shred of sanity. But I feel like I have already pushed beyond that boundary. I'm already losing my mind. Time feels simultaneously stretched out and tightly compacted. Minutes pass like hours. Hours pass like days.

I don't have a single idea what is going on when I see the dark-eyed captor's hulking figure come barging through the open door, shoulders raised, hands clenched into fists by his sides. I can't make out much of his facial expression, but I do see his furrowed brow. That combined with the rest of his aggressive body language tells me I'm in trouble of some kind. I don't know what I did wrong or what I did to deserve what he's got in store for me.

I'm wide awake the second I lay eyes on him, regardless of the hour.

I manage to clumsily stand up and press myself as far back against the wall as possible, gasping for breaths while my whole body goes into survival mode. I have to be realistic about this, even if it's terrifying to think about. The truth of the matter is that I'm completely vulnerable here. I have little recourse. If this man is about to attack me, there is very little I can do to protect myself.

What will I do?

Cry out for help?

Nobody here is going to help me. That much is obvious. In fact, it's bad enough that this dark-eyed man has had to protect me from his own associates. That tells me that in the hierarchy of evil intentions, my dark-eyed captor is at the bottom— the least evil. And considering he kidnapped me and threw me into a filthy cell and left me here, I would hazard a guess that the base level for evil is at an all-time low.

He is not a good man, despite the little gifts he has given me. Despite the undeniable and confusing electrical jolt of attraction that seizes me every time he touches my body, I have to remember that he's not my savior. He's the one who put me here.

I should hate him. I definitely should at least fear him. The things he could do to me, the ways he could hurt my body, break my heart, shatter my soul… well, I should know better than to let myself feel anything warmer than ice-cold hatred for him.

And yet when he first comes hurtling at me, my first instinct is not to defend myself, it's to rush into his arms. A split-second flash of longing, the image in my mind of his powerful arms wrapped comfortingly around my much smaller frame. He could scoop me up and hold me to his chest. I can perfectly imagine hearing his heartbeat, feeling it thump against my cheek as his huge, rough hands stroke my hair and cup my chin.

But then, when I see the anger flashing in his black eyes, reality comes knocking again and I am swiftly, violently reminded that this man does not have good intentions for me. I have to defend myself as best I can. I can't give in so easily.

So, I do the first thing I can think of to try: I dart two quick steps away to snatch up the pencil he gifted me earlier, from where it's lying on top of the journal. It's an old-fashioned pencil, not the mechanical kind, and to my relief the tip is pointed and sharpened. It's like a very tiny, fragile dagger. I thank my lucky stars for whoever sharpened this pencil as I hold it out in front of my chest, the whittled point aimed out at my captor as he approaches me angrily. He glances down at the pencil, raises an eyebrow incredulously, then glares right into my face. I gulp back my fear and stare at him, trying to look as defiant and brave as I can. I know that's all I have right now. A bluff.

There's a brief pause, then he grunts in a way that could almost be a laugh. Like he's laughing at me, at my weak defense. He's calling my bluff. He keeps coming closer. Now, every nerve in my body is on fire, screaming for me to run, shout, stab him with the pencil. Anything to keep myself alive for a few more seconds. But what can I do? I grit my teeth and wait as he steps closer and closer to me, slowly now, almost like he's daring me to attack. It's cruel.

"You won't do that," he murmurs authoritatively. "You and I both know it."

"You don't know me at all," I hiss back, brandishing the pencil like it's a switchblade. "You don't know if I've done this before. You don't know anything."

"Oh, on the contrary," my dark-eyed captor says, tilting his head slightly as he looked at me, almost with more curiosity than rage. "I know so much about you. Too much. Everything."

"Then you know my father trained me never to throw a fight," I whisper.

He scoffs. "Your father would sooner throw you to the dogs himself," he says, every word dripping with pure venom. My heart begins to pound.

"Don't talk about him that way. It's not true. My father loves me," I insist.

I hold out the pencil even farther, warning him to keep back. The captor lifts both hands in mock surrender, smirking at the tip of the pencil, held in my visibly trembling hand. Now that his arms are up and my eyes are adjusting to the dim lighting, I can see that his shirt is torn, revealing strips of bare skin and the hints of rippling muscle beneath. His biceps bulge, and when I glance over at the long shadow he casts behind himself that he looks absolutely monstrous compared to me. Like he's some mystical beast and I'm some fairytale waif, about to land myself in some tragic moral lesson. And when the soft natural glow from beyond the door comes streaming in over his facial features, I nearly forget to breathe.

He does not have the face of a mystical beast. He doesn't look like a monster at all, or even a villain. He looks like a damn menswear model, with his sharp cheekbones, angular jawline, and perfect physique, evident even in the darkness and under his clothes. I shiver, realizing for the first time that danger can be beautiful to the eye.

And then another, even darker thought occurs to me: I have officially seen his face now. I've watched enough true crime television to know what that means. If I've seen his face, I could potentially identify him to the police. Which means I'm a liability. I'm a risk.

He will have to kill me.

"And here I thought you were a good girl," my captor purrs, his voice soft and sharp at the same time somehow. "I thought you were going to behave."

"I've done everything you want. I-I don't scream. I don't fight back. I've been a model prisoner. And for what? You said I would get out of here soon, but you lied. You just wanted to give me false hope to mess with my head," I accuse bitterly.

He rolls those gorgeous black eyes and chuckles to himself, shaking his head. "Maybe you're behaving, but nobody else is," he says rather cryptically.

I frown at him, still holding the pencil out in front of me. "What do you mean? Who else is there? Are there other kidnap victims?" I ask, almost breathless.

"In the past, yes. There have been many. But none so difficult as you," he says.

"Difficult?" I repeat indignantly. "How? I've done nothing wrong here."

"Your father is difficult. Our little business we run here depends on the humanity and empathy of wealthy men. Most of the time, that's an oxymoron at best. A man with that kind of money has no space left for his heart," the dark-eyed man explains.

"What does that even mean?" I groan.

He smiles faintly, sending a shiver down my spine.

"It means that your daddy isn't cooperating with us. He won't follow instructions. You may want to blame me for this, but I'm telling you, the blame is all his," he says. "You could be back home in your cozy bedroom. You know, the one with the floral wallpaper and the shag rug. That elegant four-post bed. That teddy bear you try to keep hidden under your pillow. The little moon-shaped light behind your nightstand. Wouldn't you rather be there right now? Sleeping comfortably? Without a care in the world?"

I can feel the color draining from my face.

He just perfectly described my bedroom. In detail. That tells me not only has he been there, but he's inspected it. He's explored all my little secrets. He knows me better than I thought he could. And he's mocking me. Trying to turn me against my own father. Anger bubbles up inside of me.

"So you're trying to tell me it's Daddy's fault you kidnapped me?" I spit.

A languid, beatific smile crosses his face and he lowers his hands to his sides. "He made himself a very large, very bright target. And now he's disobeying. We gave him careful instructions on how to get his precious little girl back, and he chose not to follow them. In fact, he very nearly got me killed," he says.

"He's defending my honor," I insist.

The dark-eyed man snorts derisively. "No. He's choosing ego over love. If I had died, nobody would ever find you. He needs me to get you back, but he was willing to sacrifice you to defend his own reputation. He would rather let you disappear into nothing than negotiate with the likes of me," he explains coolly.

My heart is sinking down through my body. I feel ill. Something about the way he describes my father rings perfectly true, but I'm not ready to confront it yet.

"My father is a brilliant man. A master negotiator," I say defensively. "I'm sure he has a plan in mind to get me back. He's probably setting that plan in motion as we speak."

"No. I hate to shatter your fragile worldview, Lila, but that just isn't true. If I had died, there would be no one left to tell your father where you are, how to get you back. You see, he was willing to risk that for his own sake. He cares more about his arbitrary code of manly honor than about saving the life of his only child. I have to wonder, though, would he work a little harder to save you if perhaps you had been born a son?" he suggests, taking another step closer.

I can feel my lower lip quivering, the tears

stinging in my eyes. Every word he says twists the dagger a little more deeply into my heart. I know, deep down, he's not lying.

He's not sugarcoating, either.

For once in my life, someone is telling me the truth, and it's ugly. All the dark things I refused to believe, but always knew, deep down.

I will never be enough for my father.

I will never make up for my mother dying in child birth.

No matter what I do, he will never be able to love me.

"Please stop," I mumble tearfully. "Please just… don't tell me anymore."

"No, Lila. You need to know this about him. You need to understand exactly who is keeping you here, exactly who to blame. It isn't me. It isn't any of my associates. Hell, it's not even your fault. You're right. You've been a good prisoner. But that rich daddy of yours… he's the reason you're here instead of curled up in your sweet little bedroom," my captor explains, his voice softening in a way that hurts my heart even more.

"You're right," I confess weakly. "I know you're right."

I start to lower the pencil as a fat tear rolls down my cheek and drips off my chin.

"But you," he says gently, "you are nothing like him."

"I've always tried to be like him. It's what he wants," I mutter bitterly.

"You can't be like him, Lila," he replies firmly. "You never could be. You're not a bad person. There is so much good in you. I can feel it. Makes it hard to even look at you."

I let the pencil drop to the ground and cradle my face in my hands, my shoulders starting to shake with sobs. "This feels like a very bad dream," I mumble between sobs. "Please tell me I'm asleep. I have to wake up. It'll all go away if I can just wake up."

"You're not sleeping, little girl. You're wide awake. This is real," he says.

I shake my head violently. "No. No, no. Please. Please, tell me how to wake up. I can't take it. I can't — I can't be here anymore. And Daddy— I don't want to know. Please tell me it's not true. Please. I need to believe that he loves me," I choke out, whimpering.

My captor stares at me, totally still, as though he's not sure how to deal with my sudden show of emotions. My body is wracked with sobs as I step closer to him. I'm shivering all over, and right now I am desperate for something, someone to hold onto while my precariously-dangling world comes tumbling down all around me.

So I walk straight into the arms of my predator.

Without stopping to even consider the danger, I

bury my face in his chest, reaching up to wrap my arms around his neck, trembling with cold and sorrow. At first, I can tell that he's confused. I doubt he has ever had a victim try to touch him this way before. I cling to him, needing some kind of magical reassurance I doubt he can offer, but he's all I have right now. The only constant, the closest to comfort I can hope for at the moment.

Finally, he lowers his arms down around me and I sigh, letting my tears stain his shirt while his hands slowly move up and down my back. He's soothing me as best he knows how. This is clearly not his usual wheelhouse, but his body is warm and his arms strong. When he walks backward a few steps to the rudimentary pile of clothes and old rags I've been using as a resting spot in the corner of the room, he slowly sits down. I stand in front of him for a moment, swaying slightly from side to side, dizzy with grief and loneliness. He watches me, almost warily, like he's afraid of what I might do.

It's a legitimate fear.

Because through my sheen of tears, I do the only thing I can think to comfort myself. I lower myself down, wriggling into his lap like a child. I curl up against his chest, my fingers toying with the tear in the fabric. My cheek rests over his heart, and I can hear it quicken slightly when I touch his bare skin through the rip in his shirt. I tilt my head back to gaze into those black eyes, and I'm startled to find a hint of softness there.

For me?

But then it's like we've gone too far, because suddenly he pulls back, shaking his head. My heart aches. "I need to stand guard out there," he insists.

But I only cling to him more tightly, desperation in my voice. "No! Stay! Please, stay with me. I beg you. Don't leave me all alone tonight. I-I need you. Please, I can't be alone all night. Promise me, please. Promise me you'll stay with me."

An hour later, she's curled up against my side, sleeping like a rock.

I don't know how I let her talk me into this. You'd think of all people, a prisoner ought to be the one kind of person it's easy not to be swayed by, but it was hard to look into those shimmering eyes and turn a cold shoulder to her. Speaking of, it was going to be a cold night. I'm probably the warmest thing she's gotten to hold onto since she's been here.

I don't normally have this much sympathy for the targets we take.

Then again, we normally don't have the same kind of problems with getting our payments. I look down at her sleeping form, watching her body breathe slowly and rhythmically while her head rests against my shoulder, using my muscles like a warm pillow. What happened earlier tonight was unusual, to say the least. The second most parents realized their precious daughters were gone, they'd freak and scramble to cough up some money, even when they plan on going to the police afterward. The most important thing to them is always getting their girls back safe.

I wasn't trying to intimidate Lila earlier when I told her she'd be in hot water if I'd been killed by the assassin her father sent. If Ryder and I had gotten gunned down, I legitimately don't know what the others would have done, but most likely they'd have just turned tail and run off, disappearing into the countryside. They certainly wouldn't have tried to contact Lila's dad again. Killing me would have had the opposite effect of getting closer to Lila, and a man like Edward Hawthorne *has* to know that.

It doesn't make any sense. Well, doesn't make sense if you assume Lila's dad is a good parent, anyway. And I never make that assumption anymore.

I watch Lila sleep for so long that I lose track of time. I'm good at sitting still, and I don't want to get up and disturb her, so I stay put. But even though I don't sincerely think she would try anything stupid if she had the chance, I don't plan on sleeping tonight. Better safe than sorry. Besides, I want to keep an eye on the door too, just on the off-chance Ryder mistakenly thinks the door is unguarded.

I hate thinking about my best friend like that, but apparently, it's goddamn necessary.

Ryder and I went to high school together. We were trouble then, and we're trouble now, but he's always been smart enough to stay in his lane. He usually doesn't disobey me, but now that he's trying this bullshit, I have to hit him hard to make sure he doesn't think he can get away with it.

Considering all the circumstances, I'm surprised Lila is sleeping as peacefully as she is.

She stirs in her sleep, but instead of waking up, she just slides her arms around mine. I arch an eyebrow as I realize she's hugging my bicep. She smiles and murmurs in her sleep, and I let my head rest against the wall, staring up at the ceiling and taking a deep, silent breath.

She must feel safe.

I know, because I've seen her sleep before.

Kidnapping someone doesn't mean just running up to a random young woman and grabbing her off the street. That's not what it means for us, anyway. If we did that, we would have lasted about five hours into our careers as kidnappers before it all came unraveling around us.

No, I do my homework when we find a good potential target. That means watching them for a long time before we make a move, casing the house and memorizing the target's habits. It feels wrong in some ways, but it's necessary— I probably know Lila better than most of her friends.

I know that she always has nightmares when she sleeps in her bed at home, and it wakes her up around 3am every now and then. She sleeps with a teddy bear that she seems to have had for a long time, judging by how worn out and loved it is. She hides it when her friend Cassandra comes over. She also hides the nightlight she keeps in the outlet behind her nightstand, just bright enough that she can see it but that it's easy to miss.

The little details about her life have been filling my mind for the past few weeks while we prepared for this job.

Lila's class schedule is tight, and it stresses her out, but she somehow manages to pull it all together and hit every one of them, never skipping even when she's sick. She's a chronic overachiever. It's funny, she's exactly the kind of preppy straight-laced girl I would have rolled my eyes at in high school.

The thought of the two of us being in high school together makes my heart do a somersault, and I change my train of thought.

I also know about her photography. That was an interesting one to study, partly because a photography shoot at a remote location would have been another good time to grab her. But there was something to be said about the way she went about executing the hobby, too. She always seemed to get praised for good technical skill, but she gets told that there's something missing in the inspiration side of things.

She's the kind of person who's great at getting good grades, but she's so focused on that she can miss the forest for the trees, so to speak.

All that amounts to a very anxious person. At first, I was reluctant to settle on her as a mark, because I figured she was so hyperattentive to everything that she'd catch on to the fact that we were watching her— that I was watching her, specifically. I always handled information-gathering personally. The only way to do something right is to do it yourself.

The guys have never minded. It's a pain in the ass, and they'd treat it like a chore if I tried to thrust it on them.

But Lila proved my expectations wrong. She's so wrapped up in the race that is her life that she never thought to look around her. I could have been a true stalker, and I don't think she would have noticed me for a very long time. It's strange. There was a lot of pressure back in school to be the exact kind of person that Lila had become— overworked, over-achieving, always moving, constantly stressed. But since Lila had achieved it and was apparently living it, it sure as hell didn't seem to me like it was worth the time.

If I was living a life that gave me stress nightmares on a nightly basis, I'd be throwing in the towel early. I'm not sure, but I think that means Lila's stronger than me, in her own way. That thought threatens to bring a smile to my face as I watch her sleep.

We're on the cold, hard ground in what I figured would be the most stressful situation of her life, but she hasn't stirred more than a few times, and the look on her face tells me she hasn't been having her usual nightmares. And I have to admit, even though I never get attached to the people we deal with… there's something nice about watching such a high-strung person get a little relaxation in.

Funny how she could never relax in her comfortable bed, her pretty sheets and happy dog keeping her company, but she feels safe in my arms.

I frown at myself, rolling my eyes. Damn, Chains, get your shit together. This is a kidnapping, not a therapy session.

She stirs again, and I glance over to see that her sweater has slipped off her shoulder. It's oversized, and the collar is already stretched out. I can see the top of her bra all the way down to her ribcage, and I watch the goosebumps prick up as the cold air touches it. I worry that the cold will wake her up, so I carefully reach down and take the collar between my thumb and forefinger. Slowly, I lift it back up over her shoulder to cover it up. In response, she shifts a little, looking even more cozy than before as she snuggles against me.

I realize how cold she must be without a blanket, and she seems to be in a deep sleep, so I slowly slide my hand around to wrap around her hip. I can cover a lot of her waist with my big, heavy hand. As I give her a gentle squeeze to let her cozy up against me, she lets out a soft moan in her sleep that turns into a sigh against my bicep.

Despite myself, I can't help but smile at that. Making someone feel safe isn't something I get to do in this line of work very often. Ever, actually. We kind of do the exact opposite on a regular basis.

It's not like I started doing this in hopes of being a hero, but it's nice to have a change in pace now and then.

So nice, in fact, that I even find myself more relaxed than I expected to be. I rest my head back, staring at the slat to the open air outside. Slowly, I find my own breathing getting steadier and more rhythmic, and finally, sleep overtakes me before I can stop it.

I spend the night with Lila sleeping against me.

Before I realize that's happened, the feeling of something pushing against my thigh wakes me up. My body doesn't move, but my eyes spring open to see morning light filtering through the food window in the door. They then flit over to Lila, who has her hand on my thigh as she pushes herself to her feet.

She's looking at me, and she looks shocked— she must have just woken up as well.

"Oh! Um, sorry," she stammers as she stands up and takes a step back.

"You must sleep like a rock," I say.

"Did I…spend the night like that?" she asks, brushing her hair out of her eyes and looking around as if waking up from a dream, but not a nightmare. There's a faint blush on her cheeks that I almost want to ask about.

"You dozed. I stayed."

"Oh my god, I'm sorry," she said. Apologizing to her captor isn't something I normally expect, but it's not that surprising from her.

"For what?" I grunt.

"I've just…never really slept with a guy before," she says with a nervous laugh, and her blush grows.

"Yeah, I guess we did sleep together, didn't we?" I chuckle back. "Hope it beat the floor."

"I have to admit, it was a better sleep than I usually get," she admits, biting her lip. "I can't remember the last time I woke up feeling well rested."

I cross my arms, still sitting, and I cock my head to the side, peering into her.

"You live a pretty high stress life. This is the first time in a while you've gotten a night's sleep without having to worry about your own responsibilities the next morning. You don't have the weight of your whole life waiting to come after you as soon as you climb out of bed."

"That's…insightful," she says with some hesitation, and I can hear the word *surprisingly* unspoken behind her lips.

I smile at her casually.

"Just treat this like a vacation. Easy."

She laughs softly, but she looks ashamed of herself for doing so.

"I'm serious," I say, losing a little of my gruff edge I've been maintaining— and I barely notice that I do so. "Think about it. How does it make you feel, having that burden off your shoulders for a second? Knowing you can't fuck things up for once in your life? That you're not in control of whether you succeed or fail?"

She hesitates for a longer moment, and I think I might have touched on something she wasn't expecting to have to confront this soon after waking up.

"Feeling powerless?" she says. "No, not really- I mean, maybe."

She's wrestling with something, and she tries to change the subject.

"Can I ask you a question?"

"Shoot," I say as I peer up at her.

"What's your name?"

"Call me Chains."

She gives me a look that tells me she knows that's

not my real name. That's obvious, but it doesn't make a difference. I stand up slowly, and I see that faint blush cross her cheeks again as she gets a reminder of my full height.

"Before you ask, it's better if you just call me Chains," I clarify, and in my defense, that *is* what everyone calls me.

"Where are you going?" she asks as I start to walk past her toward the door.

"Need to go have a chat with your dad," I say simply.

Suddenly, I feel something warm on my bicep. I stop and turn my head to see her narrow hand on my muscles, hesitating halfway between squeezing me and holding back. I look up to see worry in her face, anxiety behind those beautiful blue eyes.

"Don't be gone long," she asks, and I can hear the request dripping with shame for asking for comfort from her captor.

I'm a cold man, but I'm not heartless. I put a hand over hers and give it a reassuring squeeze, nodding before I move on toward the door.

"If you really want my dad to pay attention," she says, making me stop with the door halfway open, "you'd be better off threatening his mansion. That old place is worth more to him than me."

The tone in that statement is interesting, caught somewhere between a bitter joke and a truth she's afraid and ashamed of. I glance back at her over my shoulder, but I don't say anything. I just let her know that I've heard her.

And with that message received, I let the door shut behind me.

I have work to do.

I reach out a shaking hand, my fingers outstretched toward the wall. I'm sitting cross-legged on the filthy floor, wearing the clothing Chains brought me from home. I run my fingers over the tally marks in the wall, feeling the deep ridges and wondering whose hands were here before.

Who was desperate enough to leave a mark in this cell as to undoubtedly destroy her fingernails to tally up the days in captivity. Judging from what I have gleaned about their kidnapping business from Chains, the last tenant here had to have been another girl. Probably young like me. I'm sure she hails from a well-to-do family. I bet she drives a sports car and carries only the finest designer handbags straight off the runway. She probably has a walk-in closet full of clothes so ritzy and fancy that she could pay off a family's mortgage with the proceeds if she sold her wardrobe off in auction. She probably wears elaborate jewelry. Diamond pendant necklaces. Rose gold bracelets with numerous charms. Rings set with ruby and sapphire. She almost certainly gets her nails done professionally once or twice a week.

I can picture her so vividly. Beautiful, waifish, fragile. Tearing her dyed-blonde hair out in loneliness here. Scraping those flawless, blood-red acrylic nails down the wall to keep some measure of her existence in order. Tally after tally, snapping her nails off, reducing her to something less pampered and precious, ruining those perfect hands just for the chance to feel some control over her predicament.

But she's gone now. Long gone. The cell does not smell of a woman. It smells like dank, damp earth and dust. Like hopelessness. I lift my sweater sleeve to my nose and take a deep whiff. My stomach churns. This sweater is from my house, but it's starting to lose that familiar scent of home. It's fading out, overtaken by the musty odor of the holding cell.

I wonder if the cell will change me on the inside, too. Will I slowly lose bits and pieces of myself while they keep me locked away in here? Will I lose my mind, driven mad by the timelessness and the cold and the fact that every surface is at least slightly clammy and damp? There is no suitable place in here for a human being to be comfortable. Even the pile of old clothes and fabrics I've scrapped together into the corner feels more like the kind of place where a dog would sleep. Not my Henry, of course. He has his own little doggy bed. I keep him spoiled and treated like royalty.

A smile flickers across my face for a moment as I picture Henry's goofy, perpetually-smiling face. His slightly lopsided jaw, his big brown eyes so full of love and curiosity. I close my eyes and try my hardest to imagine him in my arms, cuddling him close to my chest. I can so very nearly smell his fur, hear his rapid heartbeat against my hand, feel his curly, fluffy tail wagging and thumping at my hip. I can hear him panting, snuffling at my face. If I just keep my eyes tightly shut and hold my breath and focus, it's almost as though he's right here with me. Oh, what I wouldn't give to have my dog with me right now. He would make everything a million times better, I know it.

But I'm not stupid enough to believe I will be seeing him again anytime soon.

Chains made sure I was crystal clear on that.

I press a hand to my aching chest, as though if I apply enough pressure I can make the pain go away. But that's not how it works, because the pain isn't in my physical heart, it's much, much deeper than that. My very soul is bruised, victimized by my own father's cold indifference to my suffering.

Being dragged off the campus path and forced into submission with chloroform was traumatic. Having my wrists bound for hours, my body trapped and unable to move was painful. But nothing wounds me more than the stark realization that my father does not actually care about me.

He doesn't mind whether I live or die.

His own ego and reputation matter far more to him. On the list of priorities in his mind, I have never been at the top. Probably not even in the top five. I'm just a project for him. A hobby. Under the very best circumstances, he sees me as an asset. But usually, I might as well be invisible.

I think I knew that all along. Deep down, underneath all my twenty years' worth of denial and false optimism and all the distractions I set out for myself to keep my mind from wandering down the pathway that leads to the naked, bleeding truth.

He doesn't care about me. I don't know if he ever even loved me.

Of course he won't pay the ransom to get me back. I should have figured it out long ago that he cares much more about money than about me. It should have been clear to me in all the lectures he has given me over the years about how the only way to succeed in this world is to look out for only yourself.

To be selfish.

To have no qualms about stepping on the heads

of my fellow human beings on my way up the ladder to success.

I never took it to heart quite the way he probably meant for me to. I just assumed he was exaggerating, talking me up with all those awful buzzwords we learn from my business major textbooks.

Synergy. Bootstraps. Vertical movement. Invest in yourself and no one else.

I can't believe how long I've let him fool me and yank me around. All these years I've spent chasing his love, thinking that if I could only outperform all my contemporaries, if only I could push myself up above the rest, I would finally be enough for him.

I only ever wanted to please him, to make him proud of me. It sounds like such a pathetic, low-standard goal to strive for, and yet with a father like mine, it is the one goal impossible to reach. I'm realizing it now: there is nothing I could have done, no perfect path I could have followed, no amount of money or prestige I could accumulate to earn his love.

His respect? Maybe. If I sold my entire soul.

But what sort of an existence would I have to lead without my soul? I'm learning now that my soul is worth far more than what my father would be willing to spend for it. My humanity is too expensive. My happiness is a frivolous luxury, and the bill is too steep for Daddy to pick it up. That price tag is all on me. I'm cut off, and even though my heart is breaking, there's a very small, very quiet part of me who just feels relieved.

If Daddy doesn't care if I live or die, then he certainly doesn't give a damn what I do with my life. I don't have to be a businesswoman. I don't have to follow in his footsteps. I can be my own woman, follow whatever dream catches the sparkle of my eye.

Still, the realization that my only parent, the one guiding mentor of my life does not love me is a tough pill to swallow. He won't shell out for me, even though he could afford it. And when I let myself dwell on it, I can follow the trajectory of my relationship with Daddy to its reasonable end.

I can see from the very beginning how he underestimated me, undercut, undermined me at every turn. He would build me up with a kind word, only to shatter me again moments later with a biting criticism. There is no winning.

Hell, my captor has shown me more warmth and tenderness in my time in captivity than my father ever gave me, even when I was just an innocent little child.

Maybe that is why I can't stop glancing longingly over at that awful metal door. I desperately want for Chains to return. I need him to come back to me, to hold me in those steady arms, cradle me to his muscular chest like a child waking from a nightmare.

I know it's not right, the way I feel for him.

But as long as I'm in the business of swallowing tough pills, I might as well come to terms with my emotions regarding my captor.

I want him.

My heart yearns for him in a way that I've only read about in classical poetry.

It's wrong. I know that.

But then again, I am just now coming to terms with the fact that my own father does not care for me. Maybe I'm just grasping for whatever scraps of affection or protection within reach. I probably should not trust him. I don't even know his real name— Chains is obviously a nickname, and it's a rather ominous one at that. I don't even want to think about how one goes about receiving such a nickname. Perhaps my feelings for him would constitute the most messed-up sonnet in the history of literature, but it doesn't change the fact that when his black eyes lock with mine, I feel poetry blooming in my very soul.

As I sit here, lost in thought, I hear a soft thumping noise from somewhere beyond the door. I'm so jumpy and on edge that it startles me. I cry out softly and fall backward, my chest heaving. Immediately, I'm angry with myself, with my own weakness. I should be adjusting to this by now. My fear should be reaching a plateau. But I'm still afraid. I can't help it.

I need a better distraction. Even though there's barely any light straining through the open window slot in the door, I still dutifully pick up the pencil and the journal Chains gave me. With a trembling hand, I gently press the sharpened pencil tip to the page and start to write my feelings in a free-flowing fashion, much like I used to when I was an angst-ridden thirteen-year-old, hiding in my dorm room at that fancy, austere boarding school Daddy shipped me off to years and years ago.

My power has been stripped away from me. My father, who I thought was my knight in shining armor, has turned out to be nothing but a shrewd businessman cutting his losses. I am among them. I don't expect him to mourn my absence very much. In fact, I have a feeling my disappearance is just going to relieve him. He never wanted to be a father, I'm sure of it. I was never meant to be.

I pause for a moment, biting my lip. This is hard. But I know I have to confront these emotions or they will swarm up and consume me from the inside out. I keep writing.

I feel totally vulnerable. Normally, I would hate that. I would fight against it. I hate being alone like this. The only time I feel even a little bit okay is when Chains comes to me. I can't believe how much I miss him. I want him to come back. I need him to tell me what to do. I've never liked to be bossed around. I used to only ever listen to Daddy's advice. But he only ever led me astray. When

Chains tells me to do something, it feels like he's thinking of my own best interest. Trying to help protect me, and keep me safe. In fact, I would be lying to myself if I didn't admit that I like following his instructions.

It makes me feel good in a way I can't explain. It feels good to do what he says. I don't know why. I don't understand why I trust him, of all people, when I know I can't even trust my own father. What the hell is wrong with me? What is happening to me?

Why do I feel so free with him when he's the one that caged me? He was right. I feel free of the burden of responsibility for the first time in my life, and it feels so good to not have to take the blame for everything. To just allow someone else to take charge for once...

I stare down at the page, wincing at the words I just wrote out. I feel dirty just for writing them. I heave a sigh. I'm changing, that much is evident. Something inside me has snapped.

I'm interrupted by a sharp knock at the door. I sit up straight, hastily closing the journal and pushing it behind me as I look at the door, wide-eyed and expectant. What if it's him? I hold my breath, waiting, not even daring to hope. But when I see him glance through the slot, I relax a little to see those familiar dark eyes watching me. I give him a smile, which feels a little foreign and forced on my face at the moment, but it's genuine. I am truly happy to see him, for better or for worse. Crazy or sane.

Then he hands me another tray, just like before.

Some kind of fragrant stew and a hunk of warm bread. My stomach roars with hunger and I dash forward to take the tray, plopping down on the floor with the tray in my lap. I rip into the bread, groaning with delight as I chew. I look up at the window slot to see Chains still watching me closely. Maybe it's just a trick of the light or perhaps my mind seeing what it wants to see, but he looks rather disappointed. Or apologetic.

"What is it?" I ask, setting down the bread.

He sighs. "You shouldn't still be here," he says quietly. I stare at him, waiting for him to elaborate. He finally does. "It usually does not take this long. You're not supposed to be stuck in this damn cell indefinitely."

"Well, how does it usually work?" I ask, genuinely curious. I doubt that he will give up such sensitive information, but to my surprise, he seems willing to explain.

"Generally, the parents give in within a matter of a few hours," Chains says grimly. "So we don't have to hold the daughter for very long at all. These parents, the kind of people we target— they have so much money that the ransom fee barely makes a difference. It's a drop of water in the ocean for them. Easier to pay the price than get the police involved and drag things out. We only target those kinds of families. We watch them first, figure out whether they'd be a good fit. Only then do we abduct our target."

"You watched me?" I murmur. My heart is pounding, a strange tingling sensation warming the insides of my thighs. It makes sense. He knew things about my life, my schedule, my room. But I never put the pieces together that he was watching *me*. I never realized. I never felt anything was off. I never behaved any different, and suddenly I feel so exposed, thinking back to my private moments and how they were invaded by someone I never even knew existed.

Chains nods slowly, those eyes never breaking contact with mine. "Yes. I watched you for a long time. Admittedly, a little too long."

"Why?" I ask, my voice barely a whisper.

"Because you are fascinating to me," he admits. "And you are beautiful."

I push the dinner tray aside and come closer to the door, poking my fingers through the slot again and resting my chin on my hands. I gaze up at him beseechingly.

"Please. Come inside," I beg him. "I just… I want company."

He groans and pinches the bridge of his nose. I can tell this is difficult for him. He wants to come in. He wants to be close to me. But he knows it's against the rules. His rules. I don't care about rules anymore, though. I've always followed them, and where has it gotten me? Locked up alone in some dank, rotten cell in the middle of nowhere. So I don't back down. I just wait, gazing at my handsome, dark-eyed captor until finally, he gives in and reaches for the lock.

Click.

He unlocks the door and turns the knob. The metal door creaks open as I shrink back a little, standing up. I'm shivering, goosebumps all over my body. I should be afraid of him right now. I should never ask a strange man to come in. It goes against every social etiquette my father ever taught me.

But you know what?

Screw him.

Daddy is the reason I'm here in the first place. Now it's my turn to figure out what to do with my time in captivity.

Chains steps inside and closes the door behind him, looking down at me with an almost cautious curiosity. Like he's never seen anything like me before. Like I'm something brand new. Something he wants to learn all about.

"I've been writing in the journal you gave me," I tell him softly.

"What do you write?" he asks. I can feel the heat radiating off of his hard body.

"I write… I write about Daddy," I confess. "And I write about you."

"What about me?" Chains presses me, taking another step closer. I can feel and hear his breaths, his voice getting coarse and growly. That tingling between my legs only intensifies.

"Do you want to see?" I offer. He sizes me up for a moment before nodding.

"Yes. Show me," he instructs.

He's violated my privacy without my realizing. Now I'm letting him see the most private parts of myself. I'm in control, even though I feel utterly out of control.

I obediently grab the journal and hand it to him, then watch his face as he flips through the pages, reading over my words. All the while, my heart is pounding. I bounce up and down slowly on the balls of my heels, feeling almost like a child turning in an essay for class. As he reads over the pages, his expression changes from soft wonder to surprise to something... darker. I see him clenching his jaw. He's trying to hold something back.

I wish he wouldn't.

But then he just closes the journal and hands it back to me. Without a word, he turns to walk away.

My heart feels like it's splitting in two. I step after him, reaching out to lay a delicate hand on his shoulder.

"Please don't go," I plead. "Stay the night with me again. I need you."

He freezes up and for a moment I feel a flicker of fear. What if I've crossed a line and made him angry? Still, I know in my heart he won't hurt me. It makes no sense, but for some reason I trust him. Slowly, he turns around to look at me, eyes blazing.

Was it too much? Is he sick at the thought of me? Of how much I yearn to give up control to him? Maybe he's just like my father, and my willingness to be a weak, simple girl is enough to disgust him.

"If you want to spend the night with me," he says in a measured, even tone, "I can do you one better. Come upstairs with me. Sleep in a real bed."

My eyes widen and I clasp my hands together over my chest. "Please. I want that more than anything in this world," I whisper. He reaches out and takes my hand. I'm amazed once again at how much bigger it is than my own.

He leans in close, his warm breath tickling my neck as he murmurs in my ear, "But there are conditions. You will be blindfolded. And you will be cuffed to the bed. For your safety. How does that sound? Are you still interested?"

My heart is beating so hard that my whole chest aches. There are a million wild thoughts springing up and bouncing around in my mind. I know I should be scared. I know I should say no. I should protect myself. I should be careful.

But I won't.

I nod at him. "Yes. I accept."

This may be the most reckless thing I have ever done in my life. As I sit here, totally still except for my chest quickly rising up and down with slightly panicked breaths, I allow my captor to take a strip of fabric out of his jacket pocket and carefully wrap it around my head. The moment the blindfold closes around my eyes, my stomach starts to churn with anxiety. What the hell am I doing?

What would Cassandra say?

What would Daddy say?

I feel a surge of anger mixed with despair at that last thought. It does not matter at all what Daddy would say about what I'm doing. He is the primary reason— possibly the only reason— why I am even here in the first place. My capture, my lonely holding in the cell, my growing attachment to this dark, mysterious man whose true name I don't even know, it's all my father's fault. He may have gotten me here, but he has no say over what I do now that I am here. In fact, if I look back at all of my choices throughout the years, I can chart a constellation of decisions that made me miserable, all done in the name of trying to please my unfazeable father.

I am slowly figuring out the ugly, barefaced truth: that no matter what I do, where I go, who I become, Daddy will never be proud of me the way I want him to be. He will always see me as an irksome accessory. Just another trophy to be polished and kept on a shelf to gather dust.

But Chains doesn't treat me like that. Even though it would be perfectly easy for him to just leave me alone in the cell all the time and deny my humanity, turn me into just another job, like I started out, he doesn't just stop there. He could so easily ignore my cries and pleas for attention and closeness. But he doesn't. He comes to me. He talks to me. He touches me and comforts me in a way no man has ever done to me before.

I have always stayed away from men, my whole life. Daddy taught me that all of them were liars and schemers, all of them dead-set on one singular goal: to steal away that perfect innocence Daddy prizes so much.

I'm not completely naive. I know he doesn't mean some kind of abstract philosophical innocence, although that's what I'm more worried about, personally.

He's talking about my virginity. My purity. If I lose that, I lose everything about myself that makes me valuable. Whoever takes my virginity will render me pointless. He's a thief, stealing away my only asset and leaving me a broken woman. That's what I've always been taught, at least.

But as Chains lowers his powerful, capable arms around my body and hoists me up to cradle my body against his thick chest, all of Daddy's truisms and warnings fly right out the proverbial window. Because despite all the alarm bells ringing in the back of my head, I cannot deny how Chains makes me feel.

Safe.

Warm.

Valued.

Even treasured.

He looks at me with both awe and control, and I know he knows what I need. He can sense it without my ever having to voice a single word. He can just look at me and see my longing. Chains can see where I'm empty, what I need to be filled. And more than that, he's willing to help me feel less empty. He's going to show me how to survive this lonely time.

He's saving me.

I rest my cheek against his chest, reveling again in the stable, steady thump-thump-thump of his strong heart. I hear his footsteps and feel my body being slightly jostled as he walks out of the cell. He carries me over the threshold and I let out a long, slow breath of relief to be out of there.

My eyes flutter open behind the blindfold, which lets just enough light filter through for me to realize that we are, for certain, out of the dark holding cell. I bask in the light even though I can't really see it, and I draw another deep breath of fresher, less stale air. My lungs seem to swell with gratitude, and I wonder how much damage has been done to them via breathing in the recycled, damp air of the cell. Either way, it doesn't matter right now. All that matters is that Chains is holding me, and for the first time in days, I actually feel safe.

I feel his steps get higher and broader as he carries me up a flight of stairs, all along breathing in the fresher air, feeling it heal me from the inside. The air here is cooler than inside the cell, and goose-bumps pop up along my arms and legs, making me shiver.

Chains responds by holding me a little closer, a little tighter, almost as though he's trying to soothe me. A gentle breeze ruffles through the wisp-thin fabric of my top, and I flush with embarrassment to feel my nipples stiffening. They're so sensitive, responding to ever flutter of fabric and intimate breeze. I try to shift myself around in his arms slightly to better hide the stiffening peaks of my breasts but I know there's no point.

He can see me.

He can see everything.

And besides that, I know deep down that he can sense it too— every subtle change of my body is clear to him.

The sleeve of my sweater slips down my left shoulder, exposing my bra strap and part of my delicate collarbone. My face flushes an even deeper pink, as I feel like I'm showing too much skin. I can't see, of course, but all my other senses are heightened. Suddenly the closeness of his body with mine is almost too much to bear. I'm overwhelmed by his musky, leathery scent, the warmth of his embrace, the calming rhythm of his heartbeats.

I can hardly bring myself to admit that Chains is meant to be a villain. For all intents and purposes, I should shrink away from him, try to keep as much distance between us as possible. But he doesn't feel like a bad guy. He feels like... well, like my prince charming.

My Prince Chains.

It's a little unconventional, perhaps, but then again, there's not one part of this experience that makes much sense to me anyway. I'm stuck here, trapped in limbo by my own father's selfishness, so all I can do is cling to my handsome captor and hang on for the ride of my life.

I feel him reach the top of the stairs, his steps moving over even ground now. He reaches out with one arm, the other still holding me up as easily as though I weigh nothing at all. I hear the click of a doorknob turning, then the soft creak of a door opening. Chains carries me into the room and shuts the door behind us. It's dead silent in here, and I didn't realize until right this second just how much ambient sound there was outside before— the breeze, the hum of some kind of building settling, the distant murmurings of men out of sight. But now this room is so quiet it almost makes me nervous.

No. Scratch that. It *definitely* makes me nervous.

It must be sound-proofed or something.

My heart is pounding as Chains carries me across the room and starts to cradle me backward onto some soft surface. I balk for a moment, not wanting him to let go of me. I cling to his arms and let out a little whimper of fear.

"You're okay," he assures me in that growly voice I've come to appreciate.

And like magic, I believe him. I am okay.

As he lays me down, I realize with a jolt of relief that this is a bed. A soft, surprisingly comfortable bed. I wonder again what sort of hideout this place is, to have both a rudimentary holding cell and a separate upstairs area with a comfy bed. But I don't question it out loud. I'm too busy waiting for

Chains to make his next move, to tell me what I should do.

For a moment, I lie here alone, shivering slightly in the cool air. And then the bed creaks, the mattress gives a little as I feel Chains lean over me. I arch myself up slightly, hopelessly drawn to the delicious warmth his body puts off.

I wonder for a second if he's going to kiss me or something. But instead, I feel his hands touching my arms, then the sensation of icy-cold metal clink around my wrists. He grunts as he pulls me further up the bed toward what I assume is a headboard, and then he stretches out both of my arms and binds me to the posts on either side of me. My heart skips a beat as it dawns on me: I am handcuffed to a bed with a strange man looming over me.

He has complete control, now more than ever before.

I feel the tiniest prickle of fear, but beyond that, it's only longing. Anticipation. I want to know what he plans to do with me now that I'm bound here.

But to my dismay, he pushes away, getting off the bed. I feel the mattress rise again, my own weight barely making a dip. When I can no longer feel or smell Chains close by, I fuss a little, writhing around, trying to locate him.

"Where are you? Where are you going?" I ask, totally disappointed.

I hear the click of the door again and my heart

sinks. He's gone. He's just bound me to the bed and abandoned me. I feel sick to my stomach. I know there are other men around here somewhere, including the one called Ryder who tried to come into the cell and… do whatever he had in mind to do to me. What if Chains is leaving me here for him? What if all along it's just been a ploy, a ruse to make me trust him only so he could use it against me?

"Chains?" I murmur fearfully, trying to sit up in the bed more. I hate that I can't see anything. I wish I had some idea of the layout of the room. He doesn't answer. I start to breathe faster, my heart racing with panic. I start squirming in my handcuffs, kicking my legs and struggling to find some way to get loose. But there's nothing I can do. Chains has me trapped.

"Chains! Please! Don't leave me here, I'm scared!" I cry out in desperation.

To my surprise, I hear his voice still close by. He's still in the room.

"Shhh. Take slow, calm breaths," he urges me gently. "Come on. Slowly. In and out. You're going to be just fine. I'm not leaving you here just yet, little girl."

I'm so relieved I could almost cry. Instead, I follow his instructions and take deep, measured breaths, over and over again until my heart has slowed down and my mind feels clear. But now, for some reason, I just can't stop talking.

"Chains," I begin softly, "I just want… I want to understand this. Please. Why am I here? Why am I handcuffed to the bed? What do you plan to… do to me?"

He stays silent, but I can feel his presence. Warm but warning.

"This feels weird," I admit. "I-I've never done anything like this before. It kind of hurts my wrists. Is it supposed to hurt? Did I do something wrong? Don't you trust me? I have nowhere to run to. Nowhere to go. Besides, I don't want to leave you."

"Shh. I know," he replies, but doesn't lay a hand on me. I find myself desperate, craving his touch as though it's the only thing that can set me free.

"Shouldn't you… shouldn't you take off my shoes? Daddy said it's disgusting to have muddy shoes on the bedspread," I ramble, blushing. "I don't want to ruin the sheets."

Chains is silent again. I have a feeling this is some kind of test. He's pushing me. Trying to see how far I can bend before I break. He's looking for an answer, and I think I know how to give it to him.

Tentatively, I murmur, "If you're doing this because you want to see how I react to being out of control and the mercy of somebody else, well, here's your answer. I'm nervous. But I-I can't deny how I feel, Chains. I like it. I like when you're in control."

"Ah, yes. That's my good girl," he responds in a low growl that sends a thrill down my spine. I very nearly jump out of my skin when I feel his hands rubbing their way down my legs, from my knees to my calves down to my feet. He slowly takes off my shoes and drops them over the side of the bed. I groan with pleasure and surprise as he begins to massage my aching, tired feet. His thumbs press rhythmic circles into my sore insteps, then slides up and down, his fingers expertly massaging the pain away.

I let out a sigh of pleasure. I have never felt so pampered and special before. Nobody has ever touched my feet like this.

"I'm going to ask you some questions, Lila," he says evenly. "Answer truthfully and you will be rewarded. Okay?"

"Okay," I answer eagerly.

"Good girl. Now, have you ever been kissed?" he asks.

I clam up for a moment, afraid to be honest. Chains stops rubbing my feet. I moan with disappointment but he doesn't give in. Finally, I confess, "No. Never."

"Excellent," he says, his hands returning to my feet. I smile, easing into the pleasure. "Has a man ever touched your body and made you feel good?"

"I-I don't understand," I say meekly.

"Yes, you do. Come on, Lila. Think about it," he says, his hands leaving my feet.

I sigh, feeling embarrassed beyond belief, but I

answer quietly, "No. I-I'm still a virgin. Daddy always told me I had to hold onto my purity."

"Your Daddy lied to you about a lot of things," Chains says sagely. "Do you know that?"

I nod sadly. "Yes. I'm realizing it now."

His hands rove up around my ankles, inching farther up my legs slowly, teasingly.

"Smart girl," he compliments me. "I'm sorry you had to learn it the hard way."

"Me too," I admit. "But Chains… please don't leave me again."

"Why?" he asks bluntly.

When I don't immediately answer, he withdraws his hands.

I can't stand it. I need him to keep touching me. So I blurt out, "Because I have never felt this good before and I can't stand it when you leave me alone. I want you to keep touching me. I have never had a boyfriend, not even close, and this is the first time in my life that I feel— the things I feel when you're near me. And it's stupid. I know it is. I should be afraid of you. I shouldn't want to be around a bad boy like you. Chains, you're dangerous and you're mysterious and you scare the hell out of me, but I can't resist you. My body aches for you when you're gone. Please, just give me what I need. I beg you."

"You don't even know what you need, do you?" he asks, almost curiously.

I shake my head, tears dampening the blindfold.

"No. I have no idea. All I know is that I have needs and I don't understand them," I say.

"Then maybe what you need is someone who does understand," Chains purrs. "Someone who can give you what it is you need so badly."

"Yes," I murmur, every nerve in my body on fire. "Please."

His hand slides up between my thighs to gently stroke my cunny through the fabric of my yoga pants and I whimper with desire, shocked by the incredible rush I get just from that delicate touch. He begins to massage my clit slowly and I tilt my head back, moaning.

Yes. That. I need *exactly* that.

This is forbidden territory. Way beyond forbidden. It's is wrong in every conceivable way.

But Lila wants this, and I'm pushing on ahead without a moment of hesitation.

My hand strokes her warm, tight pussy through her yoga pants, and it feels better than I ever imagined it possibly could be. I can sense all the stress and pain in her life wound up like a tight knot inside her, and that warm pussy I feel through the thin fabric is the gateway to relieving it.

Part of me wants to tell myself this is for her stress relief, not for me.

That would be a lie.

I've been attracted to her from the moment I saw her. From the first nights I spent watching her sleep in her room, I wanted that body pressed up against mine, pinned against a wall, letting me take every little thing I want from it. I've wanted to slide my hand against that tight pussy and so much more the whole time she's been with me.

I want her.

I want this.

And now that she's given me permission, I'm going to take everything I damn well please from this good little girl.

She lets out a moan as my fingers brush dangerously close to her clit. I like that sound, so I reward her for it. When she moans, I let my strokes get firmer, more invasive, and it doesn't take her long to realize how to get positive reinforcement from me.

"That's a good girl," I whisper in a dark, husky tone. "You're clever. Good at catching on. Do you like this?"

Her mouth hangs open, and she gently nods her head. It's such a faint, scarce movement that I can barely tell she's nodding.

"No no," I growl, slowing my hand down. "Use your words. How does this feel, little girl?"

"It feels…" she starts, losing her voice as I start to reward her for listening.

"Hm? I can't hear you. Speak up, girl."

"It feels good," she breathes in a voice absolutely laden with shame and relief mixed together.

It must feel like a breathtaking relief to get such a dark, dirty confession off her lips, but it's not enough for me. I want this girl to squirm like she's never squirmed before.

"Tell me *what* feels good," I demand, pushing my fingers so deep I can feel her lips sliding around my fingers, wishing there weren't that thin black fabric between us.

"It feels good when you touch me like this," she whimpers with a desperate edge to her voice.

With the blindfold on, most of her face that I can see is her pretty mouth hanging open, begging to be kissed. She starts to push her hips up against my fingers, trying to get me to touch more of her, but I chuckle and draw my hand away whenever she does, leaving her desperate for more each time.

"Greedy," I chide her gently. "Didn't your daddy ever tell you not to ask for more than you're given?"

"I… I want more," she breathes with a soft whine to her voice that makes my bulging cock throb in my pants.

"That's filthy," I growl, teasing her. "You should be ashamed of yourself for getting so greedy."

"Please," she gasps, and I can tell by her face that her eyes are clenched tight. "I need this so badly."

"Do you? Just what do you need, girl?" I growl, bringing my face so close to hers that she can feel my breath.

"I want to feel more of you," she says. "I can tell you want this… don't you?"

"I should punish you for being so bold," I say in a

dark chuckle, looming over her as I massage her pussy and feel her hips squirming desperately under me. "You've thought about this, haven't you?"

"Yes, sir," she whimpers immediately, and how promptly she let those words slip from her soft, full lips gets me so keyed up I can barely contain myself. My cock throbs in response.

"You're just begging to give yourself up to me, aren't you?"

"That night I slept against you," she says in such a shaky voice that I worry she's going to faint. "When I was holding you, I...I...I was dreaming about you. About you taking me. Doing everything you want."

"That's a very good girl," I growl, bringing my mouth right up against her ear, letting my beard tickle her shoulder as I whisper directly into her. "Because I want *everything*."

I decide it's time to reward my little girl for being so good and obedient. I slide my hand away from her pussy, and she gives a pathetic little whimper of desperation. She makes it sound like I've wronged her by taking my hand away, and from her perspective, I know why.

She doesn't know what I'm about to do to her.

"You've been very good," I say as I move my knees down her body, and I run my hands slowly down her sides to her pants. "You're a greedy little girl, but you've been good for me. You deserve a reward."

"Reward?" she breathes with that hungry edge that makes my fierce heart pound against my rugged chest.

In response, I take hold of her pants and slowly start to pull them down. As I do, I watch her face get as red as a cherry, and she bites her lip so hard I worry she'll draw blood.

"What's the matter, girl? Worried about what I'm going to do?"

"I- I trust you…" she stammers, and I chuckle at how innocent it sounds. "But nobody's ever touched — seen that part of me."

"Good," I growl, stroking her bare thighs and giving them a hungry squeeze. "You saved yourself just for me."

She shudders in pleasure between my words and the way my rough hands stroke her thighs. She's more smooth and soft than I imagined, and I let out a rumbling growl from my chest as I bring my face down to her pussy. I let out a breath to let her know I'm there, and I hear a gasp from her lips— a sharp cry of surprise.

"Do you want this, you greedy little thing?" I rumble. "I need to hear it."

"I…don't know how to…"

"Don't be a brat. Yes you do. Be good for me one more time."

"Please…!"

"Lila," I tease, letting the last syllable trail off on my lips.

"I- I want you to use your mouth," she whimpers.

"Where?"

I'm being cruel at this point, eking every bit of sinful obedience I can out of pure, innocent girl I've snatched out of her home.

"I want you to use your mouth on my...down there," she finishes.

I tighten my grip on her thighs in warning.

"Your *down there*?" I snarl. "You know better than that. What is it called? I want to hear you say it. I know you can."

"My...my pussy," she finally whimpers.

The word sounds so deliciously uncomfortable on her pretty little lips, but it's exactly what I wanted. She's been such a good girl that I would be cruel not to reward her now.

So, I do.

When my tongue darts out of my mouth and strokes her slick pussy for the first time, she lets out such a pure, exquisite gasp of surprise that I can't believe I don't lose myself entirely. She squirms so much that I have to hold her hips down while I start licking her over and over again, and I'm pleased to find her wet with honey. She wasn't lying— she wants this, needs this. And I'm going to be generous to her.

My tongue explores her eagerly, drinking in

every drop of her that she gives me. It lingers a little longer on her clit each time it works its way up, and she's so tense I can feel her whole body winding up with each stroke. I squeeze her when she tries to push her hips up into my face, and I'm easily so strong that I can keep her down without even trying. She's weak and helpless in my hands, and she loves every second of it.

My tongue dives deeper into her. I don't just want to make her come, I want to make her remember it and get to know her pussy all at once. I'm going to stake my claim in her body in every way she's always dreamed of.

Her hips start thrusting up in a steady, rhythmic pattern as my tongue strokes keep going relentlessly. Feeling her soft pussy lips slide around my tongue never gets old, and each stroke gives me new little things to appreciate about her. It isn't just her virginity that excites me.

It's everything.

The taste of her makes my cock throb with desire in my pants as I taste her more by the second, and soon, I feel her thighs start trying to press around my head. I push them back and hold her down by her sensitive inner thighs, leaving her completely exposed, completely powerless, and completely at the mercy of my relentless tongue.

Her little mouth lets out steady moans of desire. My eyes flit up to her, and the blush on her face couldn't be pinker. She can't even close her mouth, and she's trying to squirm her arms against her restraints, testing them. But there's nowhere to go, nowhere to escape.

I start flicking her clit repeatedly, tasting her swollen, sensitive little nub and reveling in the feeling of absolute control over her. I can do anything, *anything* I want with her, and I'm torturing her clit with this wicked freedom.

Her body lasts longer than I would expect it to. Maybe there's more than meets the eye to this shivering little thing, but eventually, I start feeling the subtle changes in her body. There's a shift in scent, and she starts giving me her honey more generously as her whole body starts to tense up. My beard is soaked in her juices that have never been tasted before. I push my tongue against her clit and massage it while a stifled squeak pierces the air.

She comes, and her entire body shakes and convulses against the restraints and my grip. I let out a growl of possessive approval as she thrashes, and she fights uselessly to close her legs. But it's all in vain. I hold her down and keep massaging her pussy, tasting that sweet slickness as I guide her through the orgasm. When it starts to wind down, she's still a trembling, shaking mess.

"Oh my gosh," she breathes in a cracking voice. "What was that?"

I can't hold back a laugh.

"Now I know you're lying to me," I say as I stand up on my knees. "You've been bad with yourself in the sheets, haven't you?"

"Y-yeah, but…" she trails off.

"It's better when someone gives it to you," I rumble. "Your daddy never taught you that, did he?"

When she realizes that I'm waiting for an answer, she shakes her head softly.

"Then maybe you need a new daddy."

"Are you…are you going to…?"

"I don't know how much more you can handle, little girl."

"I can take it," she breathes.

A smile crosses my lips as I take my belt off and start unbuttoning my pants. She hears me let my cock out, and I wrap my hand around it, stroking it a few times.

"You have no idea what you're in for," I say in a thick, heavy husk. "I hope you know that."

"I want it anyway," she breathes. "I want…I want you to show me."

"That's not how you talk to me," I growl, and I slip my fingers into her pussy and hook them upward.

"Please!" she gasps sharply, and I slide my fingers out, tasting them and smiling.

"Good girl."

I walk my knees forward and slide my hands under that round, taut ass of hers. Lifting her up, I see her glistening, tortured, puffy lips begging for my cock to slide into it, and she starts breathing faster, mouth hanging open.

My cock presses to her pussy, and when I slide bulging crown into her, she lets out another cry of surprise.

"Oh gosh, oh gosh," she murmurs, terrified. "It's huge!"

"Having second thoughts, girl?" I growl, freezing and holding her lips like iron restraints.

"N-no," she stammers, scared but determined. "No, sir."

"That's my girl."

I slide into her, and her whole body shudders in unexpected, stunning pleasure. Even I can't hold back a groan, and that has such an overwhelming effect on her. She's tight and snug around my cock, and her virgin pussy is slick and wet thanks to me. Even though she seems so perfectly made that I can slide back and forth effortlessly, it feels like I'm going to break her if I'm not careful.

My cock is thick and long, and it sticks into her harder than I've felt it in a long time. I don't just want to fuck— I want to let myself go. I want her, and so does every cell in my powerful body. I'm lodged deep into the captive woman I've kidnapped, and now, I'm doing something with her that she's going to remember forever.

My hands squeeze her ass as I start thrusting into

her, getting deeper with each buck of my hips. I go gentle at first, because she's so stimulated from getting eaten out, but I'm not going to coddle this girl.

My girl.

That forbidden thought ripples through me like an orgasm of my own, and it sets off something primal and aggressive in me that I only felt under the surface earlier. Almost on reflex and instinct, my hips start getting more regular, bucking with incredible precision each time. I feel my thick crown diving deep into her and grinding against the innermost parts of this restrained little virgin who's never had a man touch her before. I'm throwing her into the deep end on her first night, but my body doesn't care.

More importantly, *her* body cares, in all the best ways.

Already, I feel her body start to tighten up again, and she gasps in surprise, twisting against her restraints.

"It's okay," I growl, comforting her as I buck into her. "You can come as much as you want. You've been a good girl. Good girls get rewarded."

As if on command, I feel her hit her orgasm again, and her body tries to writhe while I hold it still and fuck her relentlessly. But this time, I don't stop. I keep rutting into her, letting my body do what it pleases with her tight, unexplored pussy.

I get lost in her, and rather than letting her wind down from her orgasm, I keep the tension up. Minute by minute, I drive her to orgasm so many times that I lose track. My body leans over her, groping her breasts through her sweater. Somehow, in the midst of our heady passion, the feeling of her through the cozy clothes I brought her makes her feel just as sweet and so much more forbidden as she'd feel without clothes at all.

My balls ache. Through all this, I've come so close to letting go so many times that I'm deliciously sore, and I want to release my load all over her chest.

Imagine my surprise when I start to pull out of her slowly, but her legs slip out of my grasp and wrap around my hips. Her calves tighten as she tries to pull me back into her, and I feel an evil smile cross my face.

"You're *very* bold for a dirty little virgin, aren't you?" I growl. I reach forward and take hold of her hair, holding it with a tight grip as I sink back into her and use my other hand to push her hips up. "Is this what you want? You want me to ruin your precious little pussy? You want me to take your virginity?"

"Uh-huh," she whimpers. "Please, Chains, don't leave me yet. Finish in me."

This girl is going to ruin me while I'm ruining her.

"If you want Daddy to fill up your tight little virgin pussy…you've earned it."

My fierce rutting gets so quick and hard that I'm hardly in control anymore. I let myself go, almost immediately feeling a jet of precum lash out into her the moment I cross the limit of being able to hold back an orgasm. At the same time, I feel her start to well up around me as well, and I can tell my little girl is going to come with me.

A harsh, thick, ragged groan escapes the deepest part of my chest as I feel overwhelming relief crash through my body with the first jet of hot white seed that bursts into her untouched body. In the same moment, a full-body orgasm wracks her system, and a shuddering, whimpering cry meets my moan. Each time I thrust forward, I feel a gout of seed shoot into her, so much more than I've ever produced. But for her, I give up everything. This shy, anxious little virgin drains my heavy, virile balls better than I've ever felt it.

Every nerve in my towering, powerful body is bathed in sweet fire along with hers, and when the pulsing finally starts to come to a close, I look down to see her looking utterly devastated.

I smile.

My body leans forward, still holding her hair, and I press a kiss to her forehead.

"Good girl."

I can hardly catch my breath, I'm panting so hard. My whole body is ringing, tingling with the rush of endorphins and pleasure I have never felt before, never even imagined before in my wildest fantasies when I used to lie in bed at night.

I can feel every inch of his thick cock still inside me, pulsating and twitching as every last precious drop of his hot seed empties deep within my aching cunny. I feel strangely ravenous, desperate for it, like I have a craving for his come. I can't even begin to explain it. This is all so brand new, so startling to me that I don't even know what parts of it I'm supposed to feel bad about.

Daddy always made it sound like giving up my sex to some man would render me useless, that a man's body would sap all of my life force and innocence right out and leave me a broken doll, spread-eagled and lifeless like the murder victims on some police procedural show. But I don't feel broken at all.

I feel… whole.

Complete.

Like I have been holding my breath for my entire life and didn't even realize it until this very moment. Like I have finally been set free. Something inside me has been altered for good, that part I can't deny. I'm changed. Chains has changed me. But instead of feeling ashamed and broken inside like I always thought I would, I just feel good.

It feels like I've finally done something I should have done years ago. But I'm glad it never happened until now. I'm glad it wasn't with some random guy I met in a class at university or something.

I cannot imagine ever wanting anyone else the way I want Chains.

The way he makes me feel is something new and exciting and I find myself already aching to do it again.

Am I addicted now? His body is so intoxicating—his manly scent, his powerful muscles, his authoritative growl of a voice, even just the sensation of his broad hands sliding down my lithe frame. It's all so much more than I ever bargained for, and now that I've tasted the kind of pleasure he can offer me, I don't think I can ever go back.

Not that I'd even want to.

Chains leans over me to plant a soft, reassuring kiss against my lips. I arch up to meet him eagerly, desperate to keep him close. I try to gently nip at his lower lip, and he cups my face in both of his huge hands. His thumbs trace circles around the balls of my cheeks while he chuckles grimly. I can feel his eyes burning into my face, even though I still can't see anything at all through the damn blindfold. Part of me wishes he would take the blindfold off.

I want to see him so badly. I want to know what his face looks like when he's lost in the throes of pleasure. I want to see that devilish smirk on his face when he makes me feel so good I can't even stand it. I want to watch that muscle tensing in his jaw when he comes.

I know it's there.

I am learning his tiny mannerisms, making note of them and scribbling them into my mental diary as quickly as I can, like I'm some wildlife enthusiast on a forest path. Chains is endlessly intriguing to me. I long to understand what makes him tick. He knows my body so well, so intuitively. Like I was designed specifically for his use. That thought makes me tremble with desire. I want him again. And again and again. I have a feeling this need will never stop. This is a hunger that can never be sated, a thirst impossible to slake.

I will always arch toward him and follow after him, trailing around like a lost little girl. I just hope he is willing to let me stay close. I need him to show me the world through his eyes. I know he has so much to teach me, and I am eager to learn.

"Are you going to keep me tied up here all night?" I ask timidly.

He bends to kiss my cheek, dragging his lips over to whisper in my ear. I shudder with ticklish delight as he murmurs, "Yes. But if you're a very good girl, if you behave the way you're supposed to, you will get a special reward."

I can't help but smile. "I'll do whatever you want. Anything. I'll be good, I promise."

"Perfect. That's what I like to hear," he growls, letting his teeth barely graze my soft earlobe. I bite my lip and shiver, trying to roll my body toward him. I feel like some kind of flower, arching forever toward the life-giving warmth of the sun. But there's a pain I can't deny, one that I know will only get worse as time presses on.

"Chains," I begin in a small voice, "do you think you could unbind one of my hands tonight? Just one. Not both."

He pauses, and the silence seems to stretch on forever. I blush deeply, afraid that I've asked for too much. But the ache in my arms twinges again and I find the courage to keep going.

"Please. I-I just don't think I'll get much sleep with both hands stuck like this. I just want to move around a little more. And my wrist… it-it hurts," I admit. "Besides, you're going to stay with me tonight, right? You said you would."

"Yes. I will," he answers.

"Then I'll be right beside you! I won't be able to escape, even if I wanted to," I reason with him, my heart pounding. I feel him gently slide out of me finally, a gush of his sticky seed dripping out of me. I gasp at the strange, almost perverse sensation. But then I feel Chains lie down beside me, the mattress groaning a little as his weight is shifted. Is this another punishment? I start to get frantic.

"Please, sir. You can… you can throw out my clothes. Hide them from me so I can't put them on. I won't be able to get very far running off naked in the dark, will I?" I suggest.

I feel him smiling again.

"You *have* been a very good girl," Chains says slowly. I can tell he's trying to size me up, weigh out the risks. Finally, he reaches up and unclinks my right hand, the handcuff falling onto the pillow. I let out a sigh of relief, immediately pulling my arm in close to my chest. The muscles ache terribly, but it's still leagues more comfortable than before. Then, to my surprise, he undoes the other one, too. I get a split second of intense relief before he tugs my sweater up over my head, then pulls off the rest of my clothes. I lie panting on the bed confusedly while Chains disappears for a moment with my clothing. When he returns, I feel him climb back onto the bed, the mattress squeaking.

He reaches up, grasping one of my arms, and handcuffs my right hand again. I sigh, accepting my fate. Still, one is better than both, I have to remind myself. And when Chains curls his strong, powerful body around mine under the sheets, all my worries simply melt away. I wriggle up close to him, breathing in his warmth and his musky scent, comforted by his presence. As long as he is around, no harm can come to me. I know Chains will protect me.

Even with my wrist cuffed, it's not long before my body starts to relax. I realize just how exhausted I am. With Chains clasping me to his chest, I drift off to sleep.

~

When I wake up hours and hours later, I'm immediately disappointed to find that I am now all alone in the bed. My right hand is still cuffed to the post and the left one is tingling with pins and needles underneath my head.

Chains is nowhere to be found.

There is a new development, though: I must have wiggled around a lot in my sleep, because the blindfold has been loosened slightly. It's still blocking out most of my line of vision, but it's slipped down just enough for me to see tiny slivers over the edge. I turn my head, wincing at the aches and soreness in my muscles, and realize I am looking out a window. It's a gorgeous sight, what little I can see of it. Tall, lush, green trees for as far as my eyes can see. I can only really make out the tips of the trees, the canopy, but it's enough to put me at ease in an odd way. Even though I have spent most of my life in cities, I have always had a soft spot in my heart for nature, especially the forest. I know it should frighten me to realize how far we are here from civilization, from anyone who might come looking for me, but it doesn't. Instead, I'm simply comforted by the quiet and tranquility of the woods.

And once my left hand regains feeling again, I reach up and tug the blindfold down to hang loosely around my neck. I blink several times, my eyes adjusting to the onslaught of light. I look around to see that I'm in a fairly basic room, sparsely decorated. It's meant for utility, not style. That much is very clear. Still, it's a million times better than being shoved into that dark, dank cell downstairs. This is downright luxurious by comparison.

However, I am nervous about being alone here. I have a deep, unabating need for Chains to come back to me. I only feel truly safe when he's close by. But he's gone for a while, much longer than I expect. The door at the other end of the room is closed, and I can only comfort myself by assuming that it's locked, thereby keeping the other men away from me while I'm in this especially vulnerable state.

I have nothing to do but wait. I lie here in the bed, feeling the warmth of Chains's body leaving the mattress bit by bit as time ticks on. I watch the trees swaying out the windows, just the canopy. We must be high enough up to be above some of the treeline. Beyond that, I don't know where the hell we are.

I turn over on my side to continue gazing out the window. It's really the only thing to look at besides the door. For a little while, rain begins to fall. I watch the fat droplets of water hit the window pane and roll down in streaks, collecting more drops as it falls. And then, to my surprise, the rain slowly fades out into a light flurry of white snow. It's beautiful, peaceful in a lonely kind of way. I shiver at the brisk air of the bedroom, thankful to at least be under the bedsheets. I can only imagine how freezing cold that cell must be by now.

Even hours later, I realize that I can still feel Chains's come sticky between my thighs. That realization makes me tingle all over.

I bite my lip, letting my free left hand trail slowly down my body under the blankets. I have never touched myself like this before, but I can't resist. I close my eyes and lie back against the pillow, lips slightly parted as I breathe raggedly. In the movie reel of my mind, I picture Chains coming back into the room, climbing over top of me. I imagine his hands pushing my thighs open and his hard cock sliding deep inside my clenching pussy again.

As I imagine this, my fingers shape rhythmic circles around my clit, sending shockwaves of pleasure up through my body. I'm gasping and rolling my hips, perfectly wrapped up in the fantasy of Chains fucking me again, showing me the kind of pleasure I never thought even possible. I imagine his voice growling at my ear, demanding to know if I've been behaving like a good girl.

I murmur to myself, "Yes, sir. I've been so good."

I pick up the pace, wanting more. I slip a finger inside my slick cunt while my thumb massages the tight bud of sensitive nerves at the hood of my sex. It doesn't take long before I'm rocking my hips, thrusting up toward my own hand, all the while imagining that it's Chains touching me, Chains giving me unspeakable pleasure.

Lost to the waves of bliss, I gasp and cry out as I come. "Chains! Oh my god!" The words burst from my throat as I moan and shudder around my own fingers, overwhelmed at what I've done. I'm still foggy-headed with pleasure when I hear Chains speaking for real, not just inside the arena of my mind.

"Oh, you have been a very, very good little slut while I've been away, haven't you?" he growls. I open my eyes and gape at him, my hand coming up to cover my mouth with surprise. I had no clue he was back already. He must have been watching me the whole time.

"I-I couldn't stop myself, I'm sorry," I tell him hastily, scooting back on the bed and preparing for some kind of punishment. But instead, there's a bright twinkle in his black eyes that puts me at ease. He looks… almost proud of me.

"No, no. Don't apologize for that," Chains chides gently, reaching out to cup my cheek. My eyes flutter shut as I lean into his touch hungrily, desperate for his warmth. I turn and softly plant a kiss on his palm, making him chuckle.

"So sweet," he coos. "What a good girl. I knew I was right to get you such a special gift. You've certainly earned it."

I open my eyes and look at him curiously. "A special gift?" I repeat breathlessly. "What is it? Where did you go today?"

Chains smiles at me, and it's such a beautiful look on his handsome face that I almost forget to breathe. Then he reaches over to uncuff my right hand, bringing my wrist to his lips in a soft, healing kiss. "Come. We'll go downstairs and I'll show you what gifts I got for you," he tells me, getting off the bed. I hesitantly move to the edge of the bed, waiting for instruction.

"So obedient. So good," he praises me. He grabs the blindfold from around my neck and slides it carefully back up, fastening it more securely around my eyes. Then he scoops me up into his strong arms and carries me out of the room and down the stairs.

The whole time, I breathe in his familiar, comforting scent and soak up his bodily warmth, feeling strangely at home. Like his mere presence is enough to turn captivity into coziness. I'm completely naked, and I know I should be ashamed of it, but I'm not. As long as Chains has me, I'm fine. No matter what.

I can smell the holding cell before we even step inside it, and I stiffen up a little, clinging to Chains. I don't want to be back here. I hate this cell. But he gently sets me down. I can hear what sounds like strange, quick breathing. Too quick to belong to a human. I frown, wishing he would take the blindfold off so I could figure out what the hell is going on. But I stand here patiently as Chains dresses me in a clean bra, sweater, panties, and skirt. The sweater and the skirt smell familiar, like my bedroom, but the lingerie is new. I can tell. I feel a little thrill of excitement at the idea of Chains picking out brand new lingerie for me to wear.

The strange, rapid breathing I hear from across the room makes me uneasy, and finally I ask Chains, "What is that sound?"

"It's a very, very special gift for you," he replies, and I feel him reach to slide the blindfold off of my head. "Something you've earned by being a good girl.

I hope it will help your time here pass more quickly and… will give you some comfort."

It's just as the blindfold slips off my head that I hear a familiar, heart-warming sound.

A curt little bark.

No. It can't be.

I whip around, eyes wide and brimming with tears, and I see that in the corner of the cell is a little pet carrier. Inside it, I see the warm brown eyes of my dog, Henry. I let out a gasp of elation and rush over to open the carrier. Henry bounds out of the cage and into my arms, frantically licking my face and whimpering. I cradle him to my chest, burying my face in his fur, letting my tears fall openly as I cuddle my precious, sweet companion.

I look over at Chains in complete disbelief, shaking my head. "How? How did you get him? Oh my god," I cry.

"I have my ways," he replies with a beatific smile. "Are you happy?"

"Yes! Thank you, thank you," I gush. "I missed my boy so much, didn't I? Oh, my sweet Henry! I'm so happy to see you, baby boy!"

Henry's whole body is wiggling as he wags his tail, clearly overjoyed to be reunited with me. "It's nice to see you smile," Chains says suddenly. "You're even more beautiful."

I can't help but grin at him as happy tears roll down my cheeks.

"That's not all, by the way," he adds, gesturing to a neatly-wrapped box in the other back corner of the cell. "I've brought you some new clothes, too. Hopefully they will fit you. I'm sure you'll look fantastic in them."

"You—you're so kind to me," I tell him, almost in shock. "Why?"

Chains only smiles at me warmly and shrugs. "You deserve it," he says simply.

CHAINS

Since I can't take Lila outdoors, I have to find a way to improvise a little reunion time with her best friend.

I don't exactly have dog toys on hand, but ripping the spare sheets up and using a little clever rope-tying tricks lets me whip up a serviceable toy shaped like a dumbbell with two cloth knots on each end. Lila must spoil the dog, because as soon as she held it in her hand, he got excited and started spinning in little circles. The room is big enough that I can let her play a little fetch, and I watch the two of them go at it like they were never separated.

I've seen Lila happy, but never this cheerful and energetic. Part of that is probably just pent-up energy from being locked up for so long. Laughing while her dog does a little half-run half-hop after her, she tosses the toy across the room, and the little terrier bolts after it like a dart.

My old instincts are still uneasy about letting her run around without her restraints, and I know the guys would be questioning me if I didn't have their absolute loyalty. But this situation is becoming more complicated and more infuriating by the second, and Lila certainly isn't the one making me furious.

When she first told me I'd be better off torching her dad's mansion, I took it as a dark joke— nothing more than a grim thought coming from the feeling that she's been abandoned or because she's been so alone for so long. Never for a second did I ever think she was serious. I assumed there was some complication on his end, or maybe he had gone on a business trip unexpectedly right around the time I took Lila.

The reports the guys are giving me says something very different. The longer this drags out, the more second thoughts I'm having about Edward Hawthorne and how much I assumed he cares about his daughter.

That's what pisses me off.

I've handled everything to do with her house directly— Ryder has been my driver, and I've been the one to actually, physically enter the house and do more work as needed. The fact that it's been so easy has been part of what clues me in that something's off.

Normally there would be a police stakeout on her apartment by now. That, or if the mark was really careful, they'd hire a private eye to do that, or at least set up a camera on the premises. But I know what to look for when I go and do this shit, and I'm positive that apartment is untouched. If there were eyes on it, I would have noticed while I grabbed the dog.

Henry was a terrible guard dog, for the record. He was practically excited to see me for the fifth or sixth time when I climbed into the window. I may or may not have started carrying treats in my pocket.

I watch the dog run ahead of Lila while she threatens to throw the toy yet again. When she tosses it, he takes off like a blur, and he jumps to try to catch it mid-air, but he misses miserably and takes a tumble that sends him rolling for about a foot before he springs back up, apparently no worse for wear. He promptly trips again on his way to the toy, and I can't help but chuckle a little. Lila is almost doubled over laughing by the time he actually gets to the toy and picks it up proudly. It's almost as long as his whole body, and he looks so proud you'd think he just took down an elephant on his own.

While Henry trots over with his toy held high, I watch how animated Lila gets. She squats down and claps for him to come back to her, and the dog picks up the pace and hurries over. He runs in a triumphant little circle in front of her after delivering his 'kill', and Lila scoops him up to ruffle his ears and kiss him on the head. It's so adorable that it almost hurts.

No way around it— the dog's cute. Almost as cute as he and Lila are when they're playing together. But I can't let my heart swell forever at the sight of them. I need a new plan.

It's easy to forget that when Lila looks so happy. After what's happened the past couple days, I could almost ignore the fact that we're by no means in good circumstances. This is still a kidnapping, and there's still a ransom that needs to be paid.

But Lila throws the toy again, and when she stands up, alone and smiling in the sunlight, I can't help but feel a pang of desire for something different. I run a hand over my face, shaking my head. Who the fuck put those thoughts in my head? I'm a guy who stands six and a half feet tall, has a beard thicker than most sweaters, and killed someone with my bare hands less than a week ago. I should not be sitting here watching a girl melt my heart and make me wish we met under different circumstances.

And yet, that's exactly what I'm doing.

I wonder if things would have worked out, if we'd met in college. I pictured myself picking her up from her place on my bike, watching her excited face in the window of her apartment before hurrying down to jump on the back, wrapping her arms around me. Complete trust. That is something I don't get to feel from a woman in that way, in my way of life.

I'm a criminal, the kidnapper, the bad guy. Lila is an angel on earth.

I want to drag her back to the bedroom and show her what kind of life I could give her. Hell, I don't even have to wait that long. I want to take her anywhere I can find space, all over this complex, in the woods, hell, even in the abandoned amusement park.

Maybe not that one. I can't tell if she's the type who'd find haunted, abandoned venues romantic. Of course, she didn't seem to have a problem with being chained up to my bed in what used to be an actual prison, so maybe there's a darker side to this girl than I gave her credit for.

Shaking my head, I snap myself out of my train of thought. As much as I like Lila and crave the feeling of being between her thighs again, letting her give up all control to me and enjoying how much she's learning she likes that kind of thing, I can't lose sight of why I'm doing this.

Revenge.

Lila might be made of pure sunshine, but her father is an evil man who's having an all too easy time right now, when I meant to hit him where it hurts. If the bad feeling in my gut is right, then he's even more evil than I already knew. He's a real piece of shit, and frankly, I'd love to get up close to him so I can knock his teeth out.

But according to Tank's work doing recon, Edward Hawthorne has gone into hiding. That's obviously not what's being advertised, but he *has* dropped off the map and left no clues as to where he might be. Business contacts are at a loss, his secretaries aren't talking, and he hasn't left a paper trail that we have the resources to latch onto.

It feels like he left us at a dead end and was perfectly willing to let his own daughter face the consequences of that action on his part. That would fit his profile, but it's so cold that I have a hard time imagining any human being would be able to do that.

But men like him are different from the rest of us. They're sociopaths with no conscience, no urge to help anyone but themselves and no remorse for things that don't hurt them. They'd take a helping hand and fleece it, then pat themselves on the back for being a smart investor.

If I need a new plan, it has to be something that'll take him by surprise.

I consider releasing Lila.

It would definitely be a shock, both to my men and to Lila's father. He doesn't have any of our identities or any way of tracking us— if he did, the asylum would definitely be under assault by more mercenary assassins by now. If we take Lila somewhere that she can't follow us back and just release her back into the world, that might serve us well.

It would make Lila's dad think he has won, which is a damn good thing. He'd think that we were just cutting our losses, that we never planned on backing up our threats, and that we were going to be out of sight and out of the area for good. That would flush him out and get him to let his guard down. Men who don't do add anything to the world are always the ones most eager to show the world when they think they've won something.

It's pathetic at best, dangerous at worst.

But there's one big problem with that plan: Lila.

I'm close to feeling like I can trust Lila, and that's dangerous of me. I can't even trust my own body here. I've got it hard for Lila, and that means I'm not thinking rationally. I have to remember that if I were to let Lila go, it would be all too easy for her to go straight to the police. She knows my face intimately, and she's seen enough of this complex now that she could probably point the feds in the right direction with a little guidance.

I can't trust my body, and I can't trust the girl I want. This is a tight spot, and I don't like it.

But then I notice Lila coming my way, a spring in her step, and I feel my worries melt away like snow in the hot sun.

I stand up as she approaches me, raising her eyebrows and laughing as I smile at her.

"Maybe I overestimated how much exercise I can get after a few days in the same room," she says playfully.

"Oh really?" I say, approaching her. "We'll just have to get you a little more used to moving around in other ways, then."

Before she can answer, I take her by the hips and scoop her off her feet. She's as light as a feather to my rippling arms, and the sound of her giggle when I lift her high makes my heart flutter. I spin her around and pin her against the wall gently, and I can see that familiar blush in her cheeks again that gets my blood running hot.

Her face is smiling and excited by the time I lean in and kiss her, and she moans into it softly. She wraps her legs around my waist as I hold her, tasting her, and her hands start to explore my sides.

Just then, I feel something small butt against the back of my knee, making us freeze in the middle of what was quickly steaming up. I look down to see Henry looking at me urgently, paws on my leg, toy in his mouth.

I can't help but laugh good-naturedly at the little guy, and I flash a grin at Lila before setting her down gently and taking the other end of the dog toy. Henry growls 'ferociously' as he starts to play tug-of-war with me, jerking his head back and forth while I hold the little rag.

"Wow, Henry, way to be a cockblock," Lila jokes,

brushing her hair out of her eyes and stepping around us to watch with an amused expression.

Henry must weigh nothing more than ten pounds, but even so, I pretend that he's completely overpowering me and tugging me along.

"He's too strong, I can't hold on!" I joke, pretending I'm using all my might to keep a hold on the rag, and Lila giggles as I finally yank it from Henry and toss it across the room for him.

I laugh, then look to Lila, who's gazing at me thoughtfully. I arch an eyebrow at her as I stand back up to my full height.

"You look like you're thinking about something."

"Oh, nothing. I mean, I'm just kind of surprised."

"Surprised?"

"When my dad got interrupted for *anything*, he'd fly into this…really scary fit of rage. I was just a little anxious when the little guy jumped up on you."

"He's just a dog," I said, shrugging as I approached her with a soft smile on my face. "But it sounds like you need a new daddy," I repeat, more seriously this time.

That took the words from her mouth, and she stared at me with a blush for a few moments before a knock at the door made both our heads jerk that way.

I approach the door and pull it open, and I see Hawk standing there, sharp eyes peering at me uncertainly.

"Hey, boss."

"Hey. What's up?" I say, feeling a little annoyed at the second interruption but not letting myself take it out on Hawk.

He's doing his job exactly the way I'd want him to.

"Thought I'd give you an update in person."

"Sounds like I'm not gonna like it."

"I have no idea, that's the problem," Hawk chuckles darkly. "The good news is, the mark hasn't gone to the police or the media, as far as I can tell. But someone has got to have tipped them off. I'm starting to see stakeouts around campus, and some of my contacts say people are asking questions."

"Shit," I murmur. "It was only a matter of time, anyway. She called in sick, so I'd think classes would be covered, but that won't last us forever. There must be someone else."

I open the door enough for Hawk and Lila to see each other. Lila has stopped playing and picked up Henry, watching us curiously and nervously.

"Lila, work with us here— is there *anyone* else who'd be looking for you right now? Anyone who might go to the cops?"

She's silent for a moment, looking like she's thinking hard, but she frowns, shaking her head.

"No, not that I know of."

I stare at her hard for a few long moments, but I

choose to believe her, and I nod solemnly before looking back to Hawk.

"There's got to be someone out there. Could be her father pulling strings through a few channels. Find that someone and take care of it."

"You got it, boss," Hawk says, and I nod, closing the door and looking back to Lila.

The girl is harder to read than I'd like to admit… and it could cost us everything, if she wants to cause trouble.

I frown at Chains, then at his associate—Hawk—in confusion. I can't exactly pretend like I know what's going on here. This is an illicit trade I have no business with, and I have a feeling the less I know, the better it is for everyone all around. But knowing that doesn't keep my mind from wandering in worried circles. The tone of voice these men use to talk about "the mark" makes me a little nervous. Okay, a lot nervous. I want so desperately to trust Chains. After all, he has done a lot to earn my trust, even my affection. I don't know if it's on purpose, but I can't deny that he earned a whole lot of points just by bringing me my dog.

Henry, meanwhile, is squirming in my arms, trying to wriggle around to better face me so he has easier access to lick my chin. I hold him close, suddenly feeling very defensive and protective of him. Who knows what kind of dark activities these guys get involved in?

And the phrase, "take care of it," has me pretty shaken up. I don't know what that entails, but I have a strong feeling it's nothing very pleasant. Especially because there's a good chance the person who's been looking for me is Cassandra. She's innocent, totally outside these guys' jurisdiction, as far as I'm concerned. I don't want them to harm her. I don't even want them to contact her or mess with her in any way. She's probably just worried about me, like a good friend should be. I mean, I did disappear off the face of the earth from her perspective. Of course, she's worried about me. As Hawk and Chains continue to exchange a cryptic discussion of how to take care of the problem, I muster up enough courage to interrupt.

"Wait," I interject suddenly, "you can't possibly be talking about dragging my friend Cassandra into all this, right?"

Hawk and Chains both slowly turn to look at me, brows furrowed, wearing identical expressions of wariness. I feel a chill run down my spine. Having both of these incredibly dangerous men looking at me like this is nerve-wracking.

"Cassandra?" Hawk repeats, tilting his head to one side.

"Yeah," I reply matter-of-factly. "Cassandra. My

best friend. I tutor her every week and sometimes we do little photoshoots together. It's a whole thing."

"Right, but what about her?" Chains prompts me softly. I'm surprised at his patience.

"It's probably her who's out looking for me," I suggest, "especially since Henry went missing, too. She loves this dog almost as much as I do, and I'm sure she knows something is up. I mean, first I went missing, then Henry, too. That's got to look weird in her eyes. And if you think for one second I'm going to let either of you harm my best friend, well—"

"Lila," Chains interrupts me, holding up a hand calmly. I pause mid-sentence, blinking at him. "Cassandra isn't even an issue. We worked that out already. As far as she knows, you're still out sick."

"But what about Henry?" I ask fervently. Henry perks up at the sound of his name.

"Cassandra believes that your father came to pick up the dog to take care of him while you're on the mend," he answers. "We don't consider Cassandra to be of any concern to us at the moment. Rest assured."

"Oh," I answer, feeling both deflated and relieved. "Well, then, I have no clue who could be looking for me. Cassandra is… well, she's kind of all I've got."

For a split second, I catch a glimpse of something like pity on Chains's face, like he's finally getting a good insight into just how lonely my life is. *Yikes.*

You know your life is an empty, sad mess when even your captor feels sorry for you.

"I mean, she may be my only friend, but at least she's a damn good one," I add quickly.

"I'm sure she is," Hawk says, thankfully without even a trace of mockery.

I relax a little, stroking Henry's scruffy head. He's panting now, staring over at Chains. He squirms a little too much and I set him down with a sigh. Immediately, the little dog goes rushing over to Chains, jumping at his legs and trying to lick him. The sight warms my heart, although there is still just the faintest worry in my mind that one of these times, Chains is going to suddenly react to Henry with violent anger. I don't know why I expect that. Maybe it has something to do with Daddy. But I have to remind myself: Chains is nothing like my father. He's a better man than that. Or at least, that's what I've been telling myself.

Although, maybe that's just what Chains wants me to think. Maybe his entire goal is to turn me against my own father. My heart starts to race. If that's his secret plan, it's working. How gullible and easily persuaded can I be?!

But then, Henry loves him. Clearly. I can't help but smile as Chains dismisses Hawk and bends down to pet the little terrier with patience and kindness. Henry, for all his dumbness and clumsiness, has always been a pretty good judge of character.

He's been mildly afraid of my father the whole time I've had him, which is strange considering how often they've been around one another. You would think by now Henry would've warmed up to Daddy, but that's not the case.

Occasionally he'll even growl at my father when he gets too close to me.

It's very odd, because normally Henry kind of just tends to love everybody he meets. He adores Cassandra, of course, which is why I often let her dog-sit him. I know he'll be happy with her. And now, he's definitely given Chains his seal of approval. Henry can hardly get enough of him, actually. How can he be a bad guy if my dog loves him so much? Surely, if Chains was really someone to fear, Henry's instincts would have led him away from him.

"Sorry, he's so clingy with you," I note curiously. "You must put off some kind of dog-friendly pheromone or something."

Chains stands up and chuckles, brushing off his hands on his pants. "I like dogs. They're honest. You'll always know exactly where you stand," he says, glancing over at me as if reading my mind.

I bite my lip. "Can I— Can I ask you a question?" I begin nervously.

He nods. "Sure. You can ask."

"It's just… why are you doing this? All of this, I

mean. The kidnapping and the ransom and everything," I ask, gesturing broadly around us.

I see him visibly bristle at the question and I realize I might have touched upon a nerve. I hold my breath, still worried that he'll suddenly explode with a burst of rage like Daddy would. But instead, he just sighs, a faraway look in his eyes.

"When I was a kid," he starts off slowly, "my father died. Cancer. Spread through his entire body so quickly he just never had a chance."

"Oh wow. I'm so sorry," I murmur, already feeling guilty for even asking.

He smiles faintly and shrugs. "It was a long time ago. He was a brilliant man with a damn good job. He was an engineer who worked on designing motorcycles. There's a lot of wealth to be gained in that industry. When I was very young, before he died, we lived a pretty decent life. Nice house, reliable car. And then, of course, he died so suddenly. We had just bought the house, were still working on that high mortgage. Then there were hospital bills. And funeral costs. And my mom, who had been a stay-at-home mother when I was little, suddenly had to get a job. Lots of jobs. She was juggling three or four jobs at a time just to make ends meet."

"Whoa," I murmur, shaking my head. "That must have been hard."

Chains nods and goes on, "It was bizarre: we still lived in that massive, ritzy house, but we couldn't afford to even buy a can of soup for dinner. We were drowning under that damn mortgage, but we couldn't afford to move either. Besides, that house was my father's dream. He helped design the place himself. So to leave it behind… well, it would have felt like abandoning my father's legacy. As soon as I was old enough, I started working, too. I barely had time for school, since I was working two jobs myself. I grew up very quickly. I knew that I had to sacrifice my childhood, my youth, to work if we were going to have any chance of holding onto that house."

"I can't even imagine," I sigh.

"I'm glad. I wouldn't wish it on anyone," he says. "And then, we were both working so much that I started missing school. Too many days. Truancy officers got involved. They came to our home and found how filthy and catastrophic it was on the inside. You see, Mom didn't have the time to cook and clean like they expected her to. For all our efforts to keep that house, we spent almost no time there except to sleep the bare minimum hours of rest required to get us back up and out to the next job. I was sixteen by then. I thought of myself as an adult. After all, I was the man of the house. But the truancy officers and the child protective services disagreed. They labeled my mother unfit to raise me, and they took me away from her."

"Oh my gosh," I gasp. "How unfair!"

"Yes. I agree. But there was no arguing with

them. I was only a kid in their eyes. I had no say in the situation whatsoever. But even when they moved me into foster care, I wouldn't abandon my mother, my responsibilities. I needed to make money— fast. I thought maybe if I could pay off the house, all would go back to normal. They'd take me back home. My mother and I would be reunited," he says, pausing as that muscle twinges in his jaw. I can tell this is difficult for him to talk about openly. "So I decided to deal drugs. I was only going to do it for a little while, just long enough to make the money I needed to pay off the mortgage and put the pieces of my life back together."

"What happened next?" I prompt him, eyes wide.

"They caught me," Chains says with a shrug. "Since it was my first offense and I was still so young, I didn't do any time for it, but with my criminal record it was damn near impossible to get a good job again. We lost the house. My mother and I drifted apart. That bank took away everything I had sacrificed for, everything I loved. I had no home to return to, and it was their fault. So, I took on a new career: one that would make me money and let me carry out revenge against the big-wig assholes who tear good people out of loving homes."

"Like Daddy," I murmur softly.

He glowers at me, and I can feel the anger bubbling up inside of him. "Yes. Like your father, Lila. That's why we took you."

"But that's not fair," I protest, putting my hands on my hips. "My father may be a little cold in his business dealings, but that's just... how it works. Daddy always says it's a cutthroat business, but there's no way around it. He doesn't try to break up families or ruin lives, it's just... it happens, you know?"

Chains gives me another brief look of pity and for a moment I feel almost indignant. He seems to think I don't know what I'm talking about, but Daddy has lectured me on this subject a thousand times.

"It's not houses, though," he counters, maintaining more patience than I expected. "These are homes. Full of family memories and stories and love and safety. Men like your father prey on the vulnerable. People like my mother who are down on their luck for no fault of their own. It's a predatory business practice, Lila, and your father knows that."

I open my mouth for a rebuttal, but then close it again. For the first time, it fully dawns on me that he's right, that Daddy's been making excuses all these years. That's what they are. Not reasons, not justifications, just excuses. Suddenly, I'm horribly disgusted that I ever listened to Daddy about this stuff. He was so wrong, and so was I.

For the first time, I look at Chains and I see the full picture of how he ended up here, how he became the man he is now. And it breaks my heart. I understand now. It all makes sense. And I can't bear to watch all that sadness building up, all that hopelessness. Without another word, I stride over to him, stand on my tiptoes, and kiss him passionately. He's stunned for a half second, then wraps his arms around me and holds me close. I can feel the shared understanding warm and bright between us. There's been a shift. We're on the same side now, for better or worse.

Our kiss is interrupted when Hawk reappears in the doorway, clearing his throat. Chains pushes back, cupping my cheek delicately for a moment before turning to his associate with a hardened expression. "Yes? What did you find, Hawk?" he asks curtly.

"It's weird," Hawk begins slowly. "It doesn't make much sense to me, but I found out who made the police report about Lila Hawthorne going missing."

"And? Who is it?" Chains presses him.

"Some woman named Sandra White," Hawk says, and I freeze up, my blood going cold.

"Who the hell is that?" Chains murmurs, frowning.

"That's… that's my mother's name," I breathe, my heart pounding. "But it's got to be a coincidence. Or maybe some kind of sick prank."

"Why do you say that?" Hawk asks.

"Because," I sigh, "my mother is dead. She died when I was being born."

Chains looks at me hard, clearly measuring up this strange new information. Then he lightly touches my shoulder, kisses me on the cheek, and strides out of the room. As he leaves, Hawk falls into step beside him.

"Wait, where are you going?" I ask, already feeling the loss.

"I'm going to look into this," he tells me, and I know he means it in a protective way. "Wait here. Play with Henry. Try not to worry too much."

I scoop Henry up into my arms and nod. "Okay. I'll do my best. And Chains?"

"Yes?" he asks, pausing.

"Be careful out there. Please," I ask him softly.

He gives me a faint, quick smile. "I will," he promises, and then walks away, closing me into the cell with Henry. I listen as their footsteps echo away down the hall. It's just me, alone with my worries and my thoughts.

CHAINS

I step into a coffee shop so cozy that I could finally understand why hipsters would be willing to pay for something besides black drip coffee.

The place seems to have once been someone's apartment that was converted into a cafe. It sits on the corner of a large building by a shopping area not far from the MIT campus, easily within walking distance for both students and office workers in the local area. Cambridge is the kind of place with not many locals— hip coffee shops are easy to keep afloat.

A few heads turn my way when my heavy frame steps onto the old hardwood floors that creak subtly. At my height, it's hard not to. That's why I'm some-what incognito today. I've trimmed my beard so that it looks a little less wild, and I'm absolutely not dressed like I normally would. But if police have any idea what any of my gang looks like, they'll be looking for a biker, and we already stick out like a sore thumb in a place like Cambridge, and I'm no exception.

Instead, I've opted for the lumberjack look. I'm wearing brown boots, blue jeans, a red plaid flannel shirt rolled up to the elbows, and a subtle, dark gray beanie that doesn't draw attention but keeps my head covered. I'm also wearing a pair of sunglasses that I take off once I'm inside, and I approach the espresso bar, eyes flitting between some of the employees.

I'm guessing Sandra White is *not* the girl with blue hair and an undercut standing behind the cash register, but I've talked my way through tougher people before.

"Hey there. What can I get for you?" she asks casually when I reach the bar.

"I was wondering if a Sandra White is here," I ask, watching her eyebrow rise sharply.

"Um…can I ask who's asking?" she asks reasonably.

But as she does, the woman at the espresso machine glances over her shoulder. She's a woman with gray hair dyed purple at the tips, and her eyes make me do a double take, because they're the spitting image of Lila's. I catch a glimpse of a name tag with 'Sandy' written on it in bright purple ink.

Asking to speak with specific employees is a good way to get yourself pegged as either a trustworthy friend or an absolutely shady murderer by other employees. No middle ground. It all depends on how I can pull off the next few seconds.

"I'm a friend of Lila's," I say.

I stop short there, and the next moment, I'm relieved to have my theory confirmed when Sandra spins around so fast she almost knocks over the other barista making his way past her. She hurries over to the counter as soon as she can without making a scene, and the blue-haired girl looks to her in surprise.

"It's okay, Bea, I know him," Sandra says kindly. "Mind if I take a minute?"

"Oh! Yeah sure, no problem, it's dead in here right now," the cashier says with a smile, and Sandra looks back to me with a searching, anxious gaze.

I nod to her calmly, and I gesture to a table in the back corner, where we might have some semblance of privacy. A couple minutes later, the two of us are sitting across from each other with piping-hot coffees in front of us, and Sandra is gripping the cup tightly to keep from wringing her hands.

"Thanks for meeting with me, Ms. White," I say politely, remembering the manners my poor mother tried to teach me.

"Oh please, I'm just Sandy," she says with a nervous laugh. "I should be the one thanking you, I-I was starting to worry nobody was…" She trailed off, hesitating and giving me that searching gaze again. "Can I ask how you know Lila, before we go any further?"

"I stop by her math tutoring sessions enough to know some of the other students," I lie, but I know enough about her schedule and who all frequents her tutoring sessions to be able to make a convincing persona of a college student who's a little late in the game. "She usually doesn't miss this much, and one of the other students has been worried about her, since we haven't heard much of anything. She always comes in with a coffee cup from this place. Said you were 'the good barista,'" I add in a lower tone and a gruff smile.

That seems to flatter Sandy, but on a more personal level than I would expect from a barista taking a compliment from just anyone.

"That's…very touching," she says, still a little guarded.

"You can tell I'm a little older than most college students," I say, looking down at myself. "And you'd be right. I spent some time earlier on doing freelance work as a PI. That's why one of the other students asked me to help. I've done a little digging, and I've got to be honest," I say, leaning forward and lowering my voice a little more. "It doesn't take a PI to notice that you and Lila look an awful lot alike."

Sandy gapes at me, at a loss for words, and I see

tears threatening to surface in her eyes. I hold up a calming hand, nodding silently, a nonverbal oath that her secret is safe with me. It confirms what I was already almost positive of: Sandra White is Lila's mother.

But for whatever reason, she hasn't told Lila.

Sandy is quite for a few moments, staring down at her coffee and watching her reflection in the swirling surface. I feel terrible having to touch on such a sensitive topic with a woman who's clearly desperate for any answers from anyone, but this is necessary.

"I've tried to get close to Lila for years without anyone knowing," Sandy says quietly. "Do you have any idea what it's like trying to sneak around to be close to your own daughter? Taking this job at a cafe just because she goes to school here is…probably both a high and a new low. I can't stand it, but it's the only way I've been able to actually talk to her without anyone getting suspicious. All because of her damned father."

There it is.

"Her father?"

Sandy looks back up at me with a more dark, resolute expression.

"Bastard. I'd bet anything he's the real reason my Lila went missing."

"Let's back up a second," I say, furrowing my

brow. "I'm sorry if this is a lot, but can I ask what the history is between you two?"

"Times like this I wish I could smuggle in a hip flask under my apron," Sandy chuckles ruefully, rubbing her forehead and leaning her elbows on the table. "I...*Edward* and I were together for a very short time. He was the last person in the world I ever wanted to get pregnant by, but it happened. It was a different time in my life. I was a starving artist fresh out of college, and he was...well, the rich boy," she said with distaste.

I nod understandingly, knowing how hard this must be for her— giving such a painful story to a near total stranger just on the off chance it might help her find her daughter. No matter what her past is, it matters that she cares right now, and apparently has for a long time.

"Ed bought me off," she says at last, clenching her eyes shut in shame. "I don't know why he wanted Lila so bad, but he specifically wanted her *without* me, and he paid me more money than I could say no to. My own mom was going through surgeries at the time, bills were piling up, and..."

I put my hand over hers as she starts to get choked up, and I have nothing but sympathy in my heart.

"You did what you had to do," I say soothingly, squeezing her hand.

"I was so scared of him, I didn't know what he'd

do to me if I refused," she said, and I believed every word of it. "He wanted me to stay away, I can only assume because he wanted to groom an heir, whatever it is rich people like that do."

That tracks, based on what I know about the kind of people like Edward.

"Bastard stole most of it back anyway, so it didn't matter," she laughed ruefully. "His family owned the apartment I rented, and suddenly, I was getting hit with fees I never expected out of nowhere. All legal. Nothing I could do about it. You know what he does these days, right? He's a banker, and he forecloses on houses that he sells to an investment company *he* has stocks in. Asshole bragged about it to me when we saw each other, and I bet he hasn't changed."

That also tracks with Edward Hawthorne.

"By the time I recovered from the blows, he'd moved out of state and must have told Lila her mom is dead," Sandy said. "The only reason I know that is because I've talked to her a few times. Tried to get as much personal chat in as a regular barista can, you know? I-I've tried to tell her who I am a few times, but there's no way to do that in a good way at a cafe. I just…the words don't come."

"Anyone would have trouble with that," I say, nodding. "Especially with a man like him breathing down your neck. Lila complains about him sometimes in class."

"That's my girl, don't put up with his shit," Sandy

said, laughing through a choked-back sob. "It's good to know she has good people looking for her."

I have to let Lila go. I realize that in one crashing wave, and it's a heavy thought I have to bear. But what I've seen here confirms it.

It will risk everything for me to let Lila go, but I cannot in good conscience keep her hidden, knowing what a rich and loving life she might have just around the corner, if she can reunite with her mother. I can probably even get them some money to disappear with, get the two of them out from under Lila's father's shadow.

The point here isn't just to make money, it's to get back at evil assholes like Lila's dad. And frankly, the idea of reuniting Lila with her mom and getting them somewhere safe sounds like a pretty good way to do that.

Hell, maybe if I do that, Lila will come around and see the good in what I'm trying to do with my life. Stealing from the rich and giving to the poor has never been a hard thing to justify, right? It'll risk everything, but my gang can cross state lines and change our names without too much trouble. And we can get moving at the drop of a hat. We'll be fine.

Lila is the one I need to worry about.

"Thanks for telling me all this, I think you might be onto something with Ed," I say, nodding. "Believe it or not, this gives me a lot to go on. I have a few old friends watching Ed carefully, so I think that might be a good angle to investigate. And don't worry, we never had this conversation," I add with a reassuring smile to Sandy.

"You're a saint," she says, looking genuinely relieved. "Can…can I ask you something else?"

"Shoot."

She looks at me thoughtfully again for a few moments.

"I don't mean to sound presumptuous, but I've been around the block a few times, and I know the look in a man's eye when he talks about someone he cares about. Are you and Lila… seeing each other?"

That's the last question I expected to hear, and it takes me by complete surprise. I chuckle uneasily and scratch the back of my neck, at a loss for an answer to what she doesn't know is a very complicated question.

"You don't have to answer, that's okay," she says, smiling more sincerely. "I've just been serving Lila coffee for almost a full year now, and she just seems so lonely whenever she comes in. It breaks a mother's heart. I can tell you're a good man," she says, giving my hand a brief squeeze, "and she'd be touched to know you were going through all this trouble to find out what happened to her, even if it does turn out that this is all just some last-minute road trip or something crazy."

"That doesn't sound like Lila, but I suppose anything could happen," I chuckle.

"Now I know you know her," Sandy laughs. "You're a calming presence, you know that?"

"First time I've ever heard that," I chuckle, lying.

"Well, that's another thing I think Lila needs in her life. But look at me, the way I'm rambling you'd think she lives with me."

"I'm not going to let this go, Sandy," I say earnestly, nodding more seriously. "I'm going to do everything I can for you two. You need it."

Sandy smiles at me with shining eyes, then nods.

"Thank you, young man."

I get up and stride away with my coffee in hand, almost untouched. This has been a lot, and it's only going to ramp up from here, I sense.

Now, I just need to break some very big, very unbelievable news to Lila.

LILA

"*L*ila," murmurs a soft, familiar voice. "Wake up."

I groan, too tired to make a coherent response. I wriggle more deeply into the pile of clothes, shivering as my body realizes how cool it is in here. And to my dismay, Henry is no longer clutched safely in my arms. Then I feel a large, heavy hand on my shoulder. I realize even without opening my eyes that it must be Chains, having just returned from his reconnaissance mission. I'm beyond tired, but I manage to drag myself up into a sitting position, blinking blearily in the dim light.

I was right. Chains is crouching beside me, a bright fire burning in those dark eyes. Henry is trotting circles around the two of us, clearly wide awake and ready to play after our nap together. I reach out and pull him into my lap, scratching him behind his ears as I gaze into my captor's handsome face. Even in this low lighting, I can just barely make out an expression of extreme interest on his features, like he has some kind of bombshell information to drop on me.

"Are you awake?" he asks, reaching out to cup my cheek.

I yawn and shrug, leaning against his hand eagerly. I breathe in his familiar, comforting scent. Musky and manly. His body puts off so much warmth. His palm feels so warm and soft against my cold cheek. I'm so sleepy I find myself wishing he would just lie down next to me so we could sleep together. I would love to leech some of his warmth and just feel safe and protected with his powerful body curled around me. But I can tell Chains is not in the same headspace as I am. He's wide awake, even bristling with energy. I give my head a quick shake to try and wake myself up for him.

"I'm awake, but only barely," I admit, another yawn punctuating my statement.

Chains stands up and walks over to the metal door, pushing it open to let more light spill into the cell. At first, I squint and hold my hand up to shield my eyes, as the light kind of burns a little. I haven't realized just how fatigued I am until recently. I need rest badly, but judging from the look on Chains's face, I'm not going to get that anytime soon.

"What is it? What did you find out?" I ask, my voice sounding rough and scratchy.

"You might need to brace yourself for what I'm about to tell you," he begins with a warning. I raise an eyebrow at him, dubious.

"Alright. Consider me braced. Just tell me what's going on," I reply.

"Okay," he says slowly. "I met your mother, Lila."

I frown at him, certain that I must have misheard what he said.

"Sorry, um, can you run that by me again?" I groan.

"Your mother. Sandra White. I spoke to her in person today," he explains. My stomach churns uncomfortably. Is he trying to mess with my head?

"Chains, that's impossible. You know that's impossible. My mother is dead, alright? That's a fact," I tell him imperiously.

He shakes his head, reaching to take my hand in a firm, reassuring grasp. "No, Lila. It's all been a pack of lies your father fed you. Your mother is alive. And not only that, but you've met her before," Chains insists.

I snort and roll my eyes. "Again, that is impossible. I don't know who you found out there who's posing as a dead woman for... a prank? Who knows?"

"Lila, she has your eyes. She knows who you are. She's had her eye on you for your entire life. She even got a job at a cafe near your classes so she could be close to you," he goes on. My heart is pounding. I stare into his face, my eyes searching for any hints of deception. Why would he make this up?

"Okay," I say slowly, running a hand back through my hair. "You say you met my mother. Sandra White. What did she say to you?"

"That she misses seeing you and that she's worried," Chains says. "She's the one who went to the police. She's the one who's been trying to find you. Lila, she's alive, and she cares about you deeply."

I get to my feet and start pacing back and forth, Henry trotting happily after me.

"Chains, this doesn't make any sense," I tell him. "No one knows about my mom. She's never been part of my life. Daddy even had her name removed from my birth certificate. He always said he didn't want me to be burdened by the past. Every photo we ever had of her, he burned or threw away. He tried to erase every image, every memory of her. I always assumed he was doing it to minimize my pain. He told me not to think about her, and definitely not to ask about her. Hell, I only even found out her name by accident once. I was about to graduate high school and I was going through a stack of old news-papers in our attic, you know, procrastinating on my final essays. And I found an article in one of the old papers announcing that Sandra White was pregnant and expecting my birth soon. Of course, as soon as

Daddy found out about that article, he had that burned, too. Before that, though, it was like I never even had a mother."

"Yes. That's exactly what your father wanted you to think," Chains says darkly.

"And now you're telling me she's been right there all along?" I ask again, full of doubt.

"Yes, Lila. I swear to you I'm telling the truth. There's no denying it. She even looks like you. As I said before, you have the same eyes. Identical," he insists. "And she's so concerned for you. She really does care."

"Okay, but if she gives so much of a damn about me now, why did she never try to reach out to me before, huh? It doesn't make any sense," I retort, throwing up my arms.

"Because she didn't want to drag you down," he answers patiently. "She didn't want to screw up what looked to her like a very comfortable, easy life. Besides, she even explained to me that she wanted to say something, but could never figure out how to tell you. I mean, think about it, Lila: how would she even go about breaking news like that out of the blue?"

"I don't know! But I just can't believe she would wait and put it off for so long," I lament. "I want to believe you, Chains. But you have to understand. My mother has been literally dead to me my entire life. The idea that she's alive, that she's been alive the whole time… I just can't even begin to wrap my mind around that."

"I know," he says gently. "I know. But it's the truth. I would not lie to you about this."

I stare at him for a long moment, sizing him up, trying to find the lie in his expression. But there's nothing. He's being truthful. I can feel it in my very soul. Tears start to burn in my eyes and I make no effort to stop them from falling.

"My mother is alive," I breathe, trembling all over. "I can't… it's just…"

"It's a lot to take in. That's understandable," Chains says kindly.

"How did I not know? I've seen her, you say," I murmur.

"Yes. You've even spoken with her before at that cafe where she works. She's the one with the gray and purple hair," he adds.

I feel like someone has just smashed me in the gut with a baseball bat. I can picture her perfectly. I know exactly which employee she is. I wish I could better remember what we've talked about together, but I never thought much of it. All just regular chit-chat. Nothing that would ever point me in the direction of realizing she's my mother.

"Why did my father keep her from me?" I mumble, shaking my head as the tears roll down my cheeks. "Why would he do that to her? To me?"

"He paid her off. He gave her no option but to

disappear. He hounded her for years, chasing her off, making her life a living hell," Chains tells me, and I can hear the hatred in his voice. "He did everything within his power to keep her away from you, Lila. He is a powerful man, and he does whatever he sees fit, morals be damned. You know that."

I know I should believe him. I know I should listen. But my instinct, deeply ingrained in me, is to defend my father. I can't help it. "I don't believe it. My father may be a shrewd businessman, but he's not evil. He wouldn't… he wouldn't do that," I protest.

Chains remains totally calm. "It's a difficult pill to swallow. I get that. But I know how to prove to you that I'm telling the truth. There's only one way to find out."

I whip around to look at him in confusion. "And what might that be?" I ask.

He shrugs and simply replies, "I'm going to set you free."

"Wh-what?" I gasp. "You are?"

"Yes," he says, nodding. "But there are conditions."

The house looks the same as it ever did.

I don't know why I thought it would be different somehow. As though my absence would show on the outside, making the topiary shapes droop sadly or that the color of the paint would be duller than usual. But it looks no different. No hints at all that something is terribly wrong, that someone is missing from the picture.

I stand in the elegantly-designed front yard of my home, staring up at the window where I know my father's office is located. I'm dressed in my MIT sweatshirt and a pair of jeans, my hair neatly brushed back into a flouncy ponytail. I don't look as though I've been through the wringer. I look pretty normal, like any other student returning home after a trip abroad.

Only I'm not returning home with a smile on my

face and a spring in my step. I'm not here to hug my father and drop off into bed to sleep off jet lag or whatever. I'm here to get answers.

My hand fumbles absently to my back pocket, hidden underneath the bottom of my sweatshirt, to feel around for the burner phone stowed back there. It feels a little weird showing up here without Henry, but Chains and I both agreed it was safer to keep him behind at the complex, just in case things turn sour here.

I can't pretend like I don't suspect it's partly a collateral situation: if they still have Henry, they can leverage me to come back instead of running off to the police. Not that I want to do that in the first place. I'm not interested in taking down Chains and his whole illegal enterprise. I just want to know the truth, regardless of how ugly or painful it may be.

It's time to ask Daddy some difficult questions.

And a lot will be gained just from gauging his reaction to my sudden, triumphant return. Every cell in my body rings with frantic anxiety as I walk up the front steps of the only home I've ever known other than my school apartment. I don't have my keys or any of my stuff, of course, since it's all still confiscated at the complex. Chains wants this to be as clean as possible, so he simply drove me to my old neighborhood and dropped me off around the corner, leaving me to walk the two minutes to the house. I lift a trembling fist and knock at the door, swallowing back the lump of fear in my throat. I stand here waiting impatiently for him to answer the door. I know he's home. His fancy car is in the garage.

Besides, I can feel his presence.

Heavy.

Oppressive.

Distant.

Yep. That's my father, alright.

I rock back and forth on the balls of my feet, listening intently for any sounds of life inside the house. Finally, my stomach starts to churn as I hear footsteps approaching. It's unmistakable: the slow, even, loafer-heavy footsteps of my father. When he opens the door, he's wearing his usual business suit with a sleek housecoat on over it, a highball in his left hand. At first, he just looks stunned and confused to see me, then he remembers to force a smile.

"Hi, Daddy," I say, following suit and hitching a smile to my lips. "I'm home."

"Oh, my sweet little girl!" he exclaims, ushering me into the house and closing the door behind me. He reaches out to stroke my cheek, tilting his head to one side slightly as he looks me over, up and down. "I was worried sick!" he adds, rather unconvincingly.

I can't believe I never noticed it before: the strange disingenuous tone of his voice when he speaks to me. It's always been there, and yet I never paid much attention. I suppose I believed what I wanted to believe. It's easier to live in denial than to admit to yourself that your own father doesn't actually like you all that much.

"Were you?" I ask, a little sharply.

A flicker of darkness crosses his face and he lets his hand fall back to his side, easing it into a fur-lined pocket. He widens his smile, but it doesn't reach his beady eyes.

"Of course, my darling. I missed you terribly. The house has been very empty without you in it," he says. "How are you? Are you hurt at all? Should I call for a nurse?"

I shake my head. "No. I'm okay. Just shaken, is all. I mean, I *was* kidnapped for ransom."

He heaves a dramatic sigh. "Ransom? My god. I can't believe those lunatics would do such a thing to you! I apologize, sweetheart. You never should have had to go through this."

"You didn't pay the ransom, Daddy," I point out innocently. "Why? I don't understand. Don't we have the money?"

He chuckles and takes a sip of his drink, then gestures for me to follow him into the sitting room off to our left. I trail after him, glaring at the back of his head as he lies eloquently to me. "Oh, of course, but I knew better than to try and negotiate with a bunch of filthy delinquents. I knew they would release you sooner or later of their own accord, once they realized I wasn't going to pay them for the trouble."

I can feel my heart breaking into tiny pieces. This is exactly the kind of emotionless reasoning he's always given me when I ask hard questions. He doesn't even flinch. This is easy for him. He was never worried about me. Not even for a second. Chains is right.

"So instead of shelling out the money to ensure the safety of your only child, you decided to call their bluff?" I ask angrily.

Daddy turns and gives me a startled expression as he sits down on the chaise lounge, gently swirling his glass in one hand. I can tell he's taken aback by my anger. He's not used to it. Usually, I just bend to his will. But not this time. I know better now.

"You're studying business, Lila," he says slowly. "You know the importance of standing one's ground in the face of a sour deal."

"So, paying to get me back was a 'sour deal' in your eyes," I surmise, folding my arms over my chest indignantly.

He stiffens up, glaring at me coldly. "I thought you of all people would understand the necessity of logical thinking in the face of illogical circumstances. One must remain calm and refuse to give into demands."

"Even if it means they could have killed me," I counter.

He pauses, just watching me. I can tell he's disturbed by the change in my behavior. Finally, he just gives me another false smile.

"Like I said before, dear, I knew they would never do such a thing. Too risky," he says. "And look! I was right. They've set you free, and I never had to pay a penny. Now, tell me all about these awful men. I want to know everything."

I see right through him. Chains prepared me for this. He knew my father would want more information. To make sure he did a good enough job of scaring them away that night when he retaliated against Chains and his gang. So I sit down on the vintage sofa opposite my father and open up, giving him the exact information Chains fed me to "test" Daddy.

"They told me all kinds of wild stories, Daddy," I begin, feigning confusion. "They said my mother is still alive. That you paid her off to stay away."

There's a moment of intense rage in his eyes, a fire so furious and bright it scares me. And then he forces a laugh which does not reach his eyes. "Liars and cheats, all of them. You can't believe a word they say, my dear," my father tells me. "They were just trying to get inside your head. And it looks as though they succeeded."

Ah yes. There's the insult. Of course.

"That's not all they told me," I reply icily. "They also told me all about your business, what you've been doing to get all this money. Causing foreclosures. Buying up cheap houses. Forcing innocent, good people out of their homes."

He rolls his eyes and takes another drink of his booze. "Yes, yes. That's no secret, Lila. That's the way it works in this industry," he says.

"So you don't deny it at all?" I ask, wrinkling my nose.

"Of course not. I'm proud of my work," Daddy declares with a fiendish smirk. "I do what I have to do to make money. Don't you like wearing nice clothes? Don't you like driving a fancy car? Well, then, you have to take the bad with the good. It may sound callous to you, but that's what it means to be a good businessman. You must be an opportunist. And now that you're studying at MIT, I have high hopes that you will grow to be an even better businessman than I am. That is my dream for you, Lila. It is every father's dream for his little girl."

I stare at him, totally at a loss. I can't believe how unashamed he is. How did I never see this before? How blind could I have been? Suddenly, a question crowds into the forefront of my mind and I know I can't push it back down.

"Daddy," I blurt out, "do you even love me?"

He blinks in surprise at the question, pausing to squint at me. The pause is more than enough to answer my question, but then he simply says, "Well, of course, I do. Why would you even ask such a horrible question?"

But there's no affection in his tone. Nothing but cold lies.

I have my truth. I only wish I could have learned it sooner.

"And now don't you worry about those criminals who took you, dear," he says, quickly changing the subject. "I have, ah, *professionals* on the job who can take care of them."

My stomach flips at that statement and immediately I fear for Chains and his gang. I'll never forgive myself if my actions put them all in jeopardy. I'm about to say something to protest when suddenly the house phone rings in the kitchen. Across the house, I hear the caller ID announce, "Call from: Cassandra Womack."

I nearly trip over my own feet in my haste to get to the kitchen and answer the phone. My hand shaking, I grab the phone off the dock and press it to my ear. "Hello? Cassandra?" I answer.

"Oh, hey! You're awake! It's so good to hear your voice again, Lila, I was starting to get really worried there for a minute. I kept calling but your dad said you were sleeping every time. What is it? Mono?" she says conversationally.

"Uh, yeah. Yes. Mono," I lie quickly.

"Aw man. That sucks. Is Henry keeping you company?" she asks.

"Yep. He's been very, uh, attentive," I answer.

"Good. Good. He's such a great dog. I wish I had one just like him," Cassandra says. "Oh! That reminds me: I got those photos developed finally. They turned out really well! I can't wait to show you."

"The photos of Henry?" I ask, a little absent-mindedly.

"Oh no. Not those. The ones we took a while back. Remember? When we went to that creepy old burned-down house?"

I freeze up. I had totally forgotten about that.

"Oh. Um, yeah! I remember," I tell her.

"Yeah, that was fun. We should do that again sometime," she muses. "Anyway, I was going through the photos and I found something kind of weird, actually."

"Something weird?" I repeat, frowning.

"Yeah," she says, a little hesitantly. She lowers her voice. "Okay, to be honest, I don't know if it's something we should talk about over the phone, and I didn't want to worry you about it while you were sick, but—"

"Just tell me. I'm still pretty sick but I can handle it, I swear," I insist.

"Oh, uh, okay! If you're sure," Cassandra says a little dubiously. "So, I found this weird half-burnt letter in the rubble. It's addressed to... well, your dad."

"My father?" I breathe. "Tell me what it says, Cassandra. Tell me everything."

"I'm probably misinterpreting it or overthinking it or maybe it's a different Edward Hawthorne, but... it's a letter accusing him of something called 'foreclosure fraud' and the letter-writer is threatening to go to the press about it if he doesn't stop," she reveals.

My blood runs cold and I glance back toward the living room, suddenly terrified that my father might be somehow listening in on our conversation. I need to hang up and get out of here.

Now.

"Wow, that is super weird," I say quickly. "Uh, hey, can I call you back later?"

"Oh. Um, sure! Of course! Feel better soon!" she chimes.

"Thanks," I reply and hang up. I stand there for a moment, just taking slow, deep breaths. I have to find a way out of here. I don't want to try and call Chains just yet. Not while Daddy is right around the corner. Our house is big, but it's also empty and silent. He could hear everything.

So I calmly walk back into the living room, wearing the sweetest smile I can summon up, and ask my father, "Hey Daddy, could you do me a favor? Those bad men still have my car, and I really need a ride to campus for… for some school stuff. It's important."

He looks at me hard, like he's trying to read my mind. Then, suddenly, he glances away and finishes his drink in one sip, standing up. "Actually, dear, I do have some work business to tend to up in my office. I don't think I have the time to take you there at the moment," he says.

I gape at him in disbelief. I've just returned from being held for ransom and not only is he not completely overjoyed to see me, but he's immediately back to dismissing me? He can't even spare the forty-five minutes it would take to drive me to campus?

"Daddy, I really need to go there. Now. Please," I beg him.

He scoffs and starts to walk away. "Perhaps your time in captivity has changed you. Stop acting like a petulant child. I said no," he answers coldly.

I stare after him as he disappears down the hallway. Tears prickle up in my eyes but I clench my fists, forcing myself not to cry over him. He doesn't deserve my tears. Or my love. Or my mercy. I trail after him, making sure to walk heavily so that my footsteps are louder. I want him to know I'm coming. I want him to acknowledge me for once in my damn life.

"Daddy!" I call out sharply. "Daddy, are you lying to me about my mother?"

He stops short and pauses before slowly turning to glare back at me. I feel a shiver run down my spine. I've never felt so vulnerable, so afraid. Not even when I was captured on campus that fateful day. This... this is worse.

"Listen to me, Lila," he hisses. "Your mother is dead. She has been dead all this time. Do not ask me anymore questions about her."

I take an aggressive step forward, holding my head up defiantly. "I have another question for you, Daddy," I tell him. "Do you have a soul? At all?"

He rolls his eyes and puts his hands on his hips. "Now, what the hell kind of a question is that? Where do you get the nerve?" he snarls.

"Here's another question: how did it feel to commit arson? How did it feel to take away a man's home? How did it feel to ruin his whole life just for some stupid money?" I accuse.

That fire in Daddy's eyes sparks brighter and I know I'm in trouble. He lifts his arm and violently smacks me across the cheek. I clap a hand over the stinging pain, staring at him wide-eyed and slack-jawed. I can't believe he laid a hand on me. My whole body is on fire. I feel like I'm looking into the soulless, empty eyes of a stranger.

There's no apology in his face when he leans in close and whispers, "I would have expected your time in captivity to help you grow up a little, but I can see now I was wrong."

With that, he turns on his heel and storms away up the stairs to his office, leaving me to stand at the bottom of the staircase, breathing heavily and trying my damnedest not to cry. My cheek stings, but nowhere near as badly as my heart does. Suddenly, I know what I have to do. I know where my loyalties lie.

I march right out of the house and down the front path to lean against the mailbox, taking out the burner phone with both hands shaking. I press the speed dial digit for Chains and hold the phone to my ear, hyperventilating. The cool air makes my cheek burn even more as I listen to the line ring once, twice, three times. I'm about to lose all hope when there's a click.

"Lila," I hear Chains answer fervently. My heart swells with affection at the sound of his familiar, warm voice. Finally, the tears start to fall. I can't hold them back anymore.

"Chains," I reply, sniffling. "You were right. About Daddy, about everything."

"Are you okay?" he asks with genuine concern.

"Yes," I answer at first, then hang my head and add softly, "no. I'm not okay. I'm ready to do whatever you need me to do now. Please just… don't leave me here with him. I found out so much more—I'll tell you everything."

I'm already inside her apartment a few minutes later when I get the text that she's on her way upstairs. Being used to breaking into places as much as I do makes you see locks as more of an inconvenience than a security system. I send her a quick text to let her know I'm here so she doesn't get scared out of her skin.

Honestly, I'm amazed this is even happening.

When I let her go, I was fully expecting her to run off either back to her father or off on her own, doing whatever she had to do to snap herself out of it and get back to her life. I already packed an emergency bag, just in case she decides to go to the police and point them to us as best she can.

Instead, she's ready to play ball, and in a bigger way than I expected.

I'm leaning against the hallway wall when she

opens the door, and despite my warning, she jumps and gasps at the sight of me before relaxing and smiling nervously.

"Scare you?" I ask.

"I might have a little bit of a reaction to tall men standing in the shadows now, thanks to you," she teases with a wink.

I chuckle, striding across the room and wrapping her in my arms before I kiss her on the forehead.

"Unless there's a SWAT team waiting for me outside," I say, "I'm glad you called me. Let's get to work."

I gesture to the table and lead her over to my open laptop, pulling up a chair for her before taking a seat myself. I have some information pulled up on the screen— stuff I've been saving for a rainy day like this over the years.

"I've heard about that property you mentioned," I say. "I looked into it some time ago. It was one of my first brushes with your dad's…uh…line of work."

"Did you…?" she asks, raising an eyebrow at me.

I chuckle and shake my head.

"This one's kind of a special circumstance, so no, I didn't get a payday out of what happened here. If I did, we might have met a little earlier. Look here."

I point out some old files I dug up tied to the property's title.

"The house was foreclosed on, but the home-owner was only two payments late. Going for foreclosure after two late payments is insane. Most of the time, it would be way cheaper on the bank's part to just keep pushing to collect those missing payments instead of foreclosing on the whole property."

Lila nodded curtly, understanding. She definitely knew more about banking foreclosure than I did, I was just trying to make sense of it from a layman's point of view.

"Unless," I say, "there's something the bank knew at the time that the homeowner didn't."

She furrows her brow, and in response, I open another page of information about a condo in development from a few years ago.

"Look here— a condo was supposed to go up right on top of this neighborhood," I say with a scornful undertone. "This guy who owned the house was the only person in the neighborhood who wouldn't sell, and around that time just happens to be when the house went to foreclosure."

"Oh my god," Lila breathes, putting a hand to her mouth.

"It gets worse," I say, pulling up an old fundraising website page. "The guy's kids helped him set up a fundraiser online to help him save his house. His family, friends, and the whole community got together and helped him pool enough cash to buy his house back at the bank auction."

"That's amazing," Lila says.

"It really is," I chuckle in agreement, "and that's what made it so suspicious that the house went up in flames not long after that."

"How did this not make national news? This is criminal!" Lila says, sounding more outraged by the second.

"The nice fuzzy part about the fundraiser online made headlines," I say. "But as usual, the aftermath didn't. Bankers get away with this shit every day, I hate to tell you."

Lila looks over the pages with a face that fell more every moment, and it breaks my heart. But it's something I learned the hard way, and sometimes, people have to see things for themselves before they get on the same page.

"The only silver lining is the obvious," I say, leaning back and crossing my arms. "The fire was ruled suspicious, because whoever your dad had torch the place wasn't quite careful enough. So, the land couldn't be sold to developers after all."

"I remember Dad being in a horrible mood for about a week and ranting about some big loss some time just after these news articles are dated," Lila says with a rim of tears around her eyes. "It all lines up perfectly."

Monster or not, it's hard to realize just how much evil your own father really is.

"The other silver lining, if you can call it that, is that the homeowner is doing okay now," I say. "But he's living with his kids and grandkids at a house they bought down the road."

"Then let's go have a talk with him," Lila says, standing up already and looking at me with a kind of resolved determination that I truly admire. "I don't want to let this go. I'm ready to move if you are."

"Thought you'd never say so," I chuckle as I stand up with her. "Let's ride."

~

There's something special about the feeling of Lila behind me on my motorcycle as we roar down the road. I fantasized about it during the first few days we knew each other, but even that can't compare to how *right* it feels when she's actually there, arms around my waist, gripping me tight as she feels the engine rumble under us.

Her face is almost touching my shoulder, and I know the autumn scents and faint smell of leather are all around her.

We passed the burned-out house a few minutes ago, deciding it was better to talk to the owner and resist the temptation to spend some time sifting through remains until we'd done so.

"Up here, on the right," I call back to Lila as we approach the house, and it's easy to tell that this is the correct place.

There are three small children running around

the yard outside, playing in a huge pile of dead leaves that seem to have been gathered up in a pile for that exact purpose. None of them can be older than 8 years old. They come to a stop as my loud motorcycle slows to a halt on the curb, though, and almost immediately, the front door opens, and an older man in a big sweater with the last of his gray hair turning white steps outside, looking apprehensively at us.

To my relief, Lila hops off my bike first, taking off her helmet and shaking out her hair beautifully before smiling and waving at the man. She's a much better spokesperson than I could ever be, so I'm glad to have her be the one who does the talking in situations like this.

And sure enough, ten minutes later, all three of us are sitting on the porch of the house with piping-hot mugs of hot chocolate the sweet old man made us while the kids resume playing (occasionally stealing longing glances at my bike).

"Yeah, I figured all along Ed Hawthorne pulling the strings in that fiasco," the old man, whose name he told us was Jon, explains. "That's not me being cynical, that's just what all of us in the neighborhood knew as plain and simple fact."

"How'd everyone get on that idea?" Lila asked while I took a sip of the sweet drink.

"Well, besides the fact that the damn condo they wanted so badly was being planned by a company he's got his hands deep into," Jon says, "he had his boys come 'round here a few times. You live in a place long enough, you start to notice who works for who."

"His 'boys'?" Lila asks.

"Thugs," I clarify curtly, and Jon nods gravely, though he glances around as if worried someone could be watching the conversation.

"They came to scope the place out, even once when my kids and the grandkids were visiting," Jon says ruefully. "Bastards. My daughter's husband thought I was crazy, but that showed him. Still, I'm grateful to the two of them— this is their house. I'm retired now, except for minding the grandkids," he adds with a chuckle.

"Oh my god," Lila breathed, and I don't think she realizes she's doing it, but she subtly moves closer to me, leaning against my side. "That's...I'm so sorry, Jon."

I feel her hand slip into mine, and on just as much reflex, I give it a squeeze.

"I'll be honest, it was a hard time in my life," he says, frowning and looking out to the kids, who look like they're having the time of their lives, laughing and screaming at each other. "But I've had a lot of time to think about it, and I don't think I can hold onto bitterness. I would be in a dark place right now if it weren't for the love my family and my community showed me. Don't think I paid for groceries for a full year after the arson," he says, taking off his glasses to rub his eyes with a chuckle.

"It looks like you have a loving household here," Lila agrees, smiling, but even she has tears in her eyes now.

"I do. I count my blessings," he says, nodding. "I've had to learn how to turn my sadness into love. That was hard, and it's even harder without closure. That burned out house was maybe a week or two of anger for Ed Hawthorne. For me, it's a lifetime of work I'll never get back."

Lila is leaning into me completely now, and Jon looks between the two of us with a growing smile.

"I don't know what brings the two of you poking around here, but I appreciate the company from a lovely young couple like yourselves," he says with a heartfelt smile.

Lila seems to realize what she's been doing, and she blushes, but she doesn't take her hand away either.

"If there's one thing my wife and I got to know while we were going through all this, it's how much we love each other when the going gets tough," he goes on. "I can see that in you two. Whatever it is you're doing, I hope the two of you have a love story that you can look back on as much as we do."

Lila looks touched, and I'd be lying if I said I'm not feeling the same thing. I squeeze Lila's hand gently, then down the rest of my hot chocolate before standing up slowly.

"Thanks, Jon. This has been helpful. I'm doing a little digging, and I'll let you know if we turn up anything that can get you that closure."

"I gave up holding my breath a long time ago, young man," Jon chuckles, shaking my hand firmly. "But I appreciate it."

"Thank you," Lila says, hugging the hold man, and a few moments later, we're walking back across the yard hand-in-hand.

Lila squeezes my hand as we get to the bike, and I look down at her as I get my keys out and she puts her helmet on.

"Chains," she says, looking up at me resolutely. "I want to meet my mom."

I sit on the park bench across the street from the cafe, staring inside at the woman Chains identified as my mother.

And I still can't believe it.

"You're positive it's her?" I ask.

"Yes," he says firmly. "As sure as the last three times you asked."

"Sorry, I just…" I struggle to find the words.

Chains puts a hand on my shoulder and squeezes.

"There's no easy way to meet someone you thought was dead," he assures me.

"Especially since she's been serving me *coffee* all these months," I almost laugh, shaking my head. "God, what if I was rude to her one day?"

"I'm sure you weren't. The way she talked, it sounds like you've been nothing but an angel."

"How could I have not recognized her?"

"It's hard to see yourself in other people."

My obliviousness still stuns me in hindsight. Chains insists she looks identical to me, and now that I'm looking at her through the window of the cafe, I can see the resemblance. Her name is Sandy, too, but I never connected that to Sandra all my life. How could I?

We're set to meet in the shop just after she gets off, which is in a few minutes— I'm just waiting for her to take the apron off so I don't make it awkward. That, and my nerves are all over the place, even with Chains sitting beside me and keeping me comforted.

A minute ago, I watched the homeless guy I give change to every now and then head inside to warm up for a moment. Now, I watch as Sandy bustles over to him with a large coffee in hand, ushering him to a seat by the window and offering it to him. I can't hear them talking from here, but I can tell by his body language that he's trying to refuse the drink, probably doesn't have the money for it.

Sandy waves it off, and I can't help but smile at how motherly she seems as she insists he sit down. There's a $5 bill under the coffee mug she set in front of him. He laughs politely and thanks her as if it's no big deal, but when Sandy has to hurry off, he smiles after her and looks genuinely touched by her kindness.

It's almost surreal.

"It's about that time," Chains points out.

"I know, I just…" I hesitate. "Wait, what name did you give her for yourself?"

"What? I didn't give her a name. What do you mean?"

"I am *not* introducing you as Chains."

He opens his mouth to protest, but he sees the reason in that, and nods before glancing around us and speaking to me in a low tone.

"My name is Chris."

I stare at him, blinking, and I feel a growing smile as he clearly looks a little embarrassed.

"C'mon, don't stare. My name's Chris Hanes. Your mom can be one of a handful of exceptions, but to everyone else, I'm Chains."

"Okay, I think I'm good to go in," I say, taking a deep breath and feeling a little more relaxed.

We stand up and cross the street, and indeed, when I step through the door that Chains opens for me, I see Sandy without her apron, just getting settled in at the corner table we agreed to meet at. Immediately, her eyes turn to me, and just as immediately…tears spring to both our eyes.

"You can do this," Chains assures me, and something about his presence gives me the strength I need to cross the cafe and approach Sandy.

To my surprise, she stands up, looking almost hesitant, but soon, neither of us can resist embracing each other.

"Lila," she breathes through a sob as we hug, and it takes me until that moment for it to really sink in.

I'm hugging my mom.

Tears stain her shoulder as I squeeze her. She's a little shorter than me, which I never expected, and it's ridiculous that that's the thought that gets caught in my head.

"Mom," I finally say, choking on the syllable.

We hug for a long, long time, then find it in ourselves to break apart and take seats opposite each other, staring at each other in disbelief.

"I'll get us some coffees," Chains offers kindly, and he steps away to give us some privacy.

I open and close my mouth a few times, trying to find words, but I can't find any, and Sandy can't seem to either. We end up just laughing at each other, and she takes my hands to squeeze them gently.

"Lila," she says at last. "You have no idea what this means to me. Thank you for meeting me."

"I can't believe you were able to keep it together all these months," I gushed, beaming. "You must be a way better actress than me."

"I did a little theater in college, but I skipped class on the days they covered how to hide from your relatives, so this is just talent," she says, holding back a big, stupid smile.

We stare at each other for a few more moments, then burst out laughing again, partly at the joke and partly at how absurd this whole beautiful mess is.

"Mom, I…" I start, "I'm sorry. Chris told me everything. About what *he* did to you, and how he lied to me. I…if I thought there was the slightest chance you were alive, I-"

"Honey, you behaved exactly like I would have if I were in your position," Mom said, and I don't know how she knew to say exactly what I was desperate to hear, but it made the tears start rolling down my cheeks in full force. "I've been keeping an eye on you as much as I can, and believe me when I say I'm so proud of you that I can't wrap my head around it sometimes."

"Aw…"

"I mean it," she says with a gentle smile. "I know what your impulse is, young lady, you're about to try to deflect it and say it was just Ed pushing you. I felt the same thing. But it's all you, dear. Ed is just…too good at knowing how to take credit from girls like us."

I can't help but laugh through my tears as I squeeze Mom's hands firmly. If there was any question about her identity, it's gone now. This isn't just my mom.

This is the mother I always dreamed I could have had.

Chains comes back with a tray of coffees, and he sets two down in front of us, picking up his own.

"By the way, Mom, this is Chris," I say, smiling up at Chains. "He…kind of made all this possible, in a big way."

"Oh, I know," Mom says, beaming up at him before winking at me. "You've got a very good 'friend' here, honey."

I blush, but Chains just chuckles and nods to the door.

"I've got to take a call. I'll check back in later, you two take your time," he says, and before I have a chance to protest, he strides out the door, leaving me alone with my mom.

"Well," I say, sniffing back tears and looking at the smart, funny, warm woman I still can't believe is actually my own flesh and blood. "Where do we start?"

"I've been asking myself that question for almost as long as you've been alive, sweetie, and I still don't have a good answer," she laughs, doing the same as me.

"I guess it would be good to explain some of what got me here," I say, taking the warm coffee in my hands and feeling it warm up my fingers. "Change doesn't really happen unless something rocks the boat, and recently…I've started to realize just how deep things go with Dad. And I need to do something about it."

Piece by piece, I start working back through a tailored version of how Chris and I met, then start working through the things in my life that brought me to where I am today. It's a long, emotional conversation that barely sticks to my memory because of how fast it all seems to breeze by, but one thing is clearer than ever now.

The kind of person I am and could be is reflected in my mom. My dad always wanted me to be him—cold, calculating, and ruthless, someone who could match up to him. Now more than ever, I don't want that, but he did give me one thing he didn't plan to.

I have the tools to take him down, and I'm going to do it— with the people I love.

The next day, we practically have a whole team assembled at the old, burned-out house.

When Cassandra's car rolls to a stop and she steps out, Lila, Sandy and the little dog go running toward her to greet her. I watch from the side of my bike, chuckling at Henry, who can't seem to decide which of the girls he's happiest to be around. The girls hug, and as they talk, I watch Jon's car approach, turning off the main road and rolling toward us before coming to a halt.

Cassandra was easy to recruit— all Lila had to do was ask, and she was enthusiastically on board. Jon took a little more work. After meeting with Lila's mom yesterday, we went back to Jon's place to level with him and explain that we wanted to get proof that Ed Hawthorne had been pulling this criminal game off for a long time, and that his help searching his old house would be invaluable.

Jon had been reluctant to dig up old demons, so Lila came forward and told him who she really is: Ed's own daughter. That got Jon's attention. Obviously, he doesn't blame Lila for anything that has happened. She was nowhere near old enough to have known anything about it when it was happening, much less to have had anything to do with it. But the fact that someone so close to Ed is interested in dredging up some justice made him decide that it might be worth the time to lend a hand searching the place.

"They've still got the police tape on this place," Jon chuckled as he made his way down to meet me.

"Yeah, the case is still technically open," I remark as Cassandra and Lila come trotting down with the dog. "Budget cuts made it not worth the police's time to close it. Formally, anyway. I'm surprised teenagers haven't torn the tape down already."

"Not a lot of people know about this place," Cassandra remarks, glancing between Jon and I. "By the way, which one of you is 'Chains'?"

Lila suddenly fights to hold back a smirk, Sandy doesn't hold back an eyeroll, and I arch an eyebrow at the two before slowly raising my hand. Cassandra looks me up and down briefly, then glances at Lila, who hurriedly steps forward to gesture among all of us.

"Cass, this is Chris, my…friend, and Sandra, my mom. And this is Jon, the homeowner. Chris, Jon, S-Mom, this is Cassandra, my bestie."

There's a moment of awkward silence among all of us as we trade nods and smiles, and I can sense that a lot of the people here would dearly like some time to talk about all the people they've just met. But time is a factor here, so I decide to step up and be the bad guy who gets things moving.

"Alright, everyone, let's try to get in and out of here as fast as we can," I say. "The longer we're messing around in here, the more likely a pedestrian is to see us and call the police."

The house itself has a sad, forlorn energy to it. I can feel it the second we step close to the place. I can still make out the individual rooms, all laid bare and open by the fire that tore through it all. The concrete foundation is obviously still intact, but all the rest looks like it's been eaten away by flames and time. There are footprints leading in and out of the building, telling me we aren't the first people to come here by a long shot. I imagine mostly kids and photographers come through here, which can be destructive, but it doesn't make this a lost cause.

Jon looks especially uneasy as we approach. He keeps letting his eyes linger on different parts of the building, looking thoughtful and saddened. I can tell he had a lot of memories here that he wasn't ready to let go of, and he might not be ready to dredge them up here today. Still, our combined efforts here are our best chance.

"Any leads on what we're looking for?" Cass asks as we step past the police tape and into the wreckage.

"Information is best," Lila answers as she walks through the house with us, letting Henry off his leash to start sniffing around. "Which makes this tricky. Any paper that was loose in the house has definitely been either burned or worn away by the weather over time. So if you can find any containers, that would-"

"Bark bark bark!"

Our attention turns to Henry, who has wasted no time wandering down what used to be a hallway and into a room past the living room. There, he seems to be circling around a burned, blackened object I can't make out, but it's large.

"Oh my god," Jon says, and he hurries over with Lila to see what has Henry so excited.

Jon stoops down in front of it while Lila tugs Henry away, petting him and shushing him peacefully while I approach Jon and look over his shoulder. Here, I can see that he's standing over a warped, half-crumbled wooden desk.

"I can't believe this survived," Jon says with a growing smile as he gives the drawer a firm tug, and it pops open to reveal what looks like a stack of folded papers. "These...this is where I kept the love letters me and my wife Helen sent to each other. Before internet," he adds, smirking back at those of us under 30.

"Why was Henry barking at them?" Lila wonders out loud.

"Does your wife wear perfume, Jon?" Sandy asks.

"Well, yes, actually," Jon chuckles. "She's from Georgia, after all."

"Henry smells the perfume," Sandy says with a broad smile, nodding to Lila. "Lila probably wears something similar, and he recognizes it."

I give Sandy a very surprised look, and she laughs, shrugging her shoulders.

"I read a lot of detective books."

Lila gives her mom a proud smile, and I chuckle before looking back to a teary-eyed Jon, who's busy fawning over the old letters.

"Can't wait to show these to Helen," he says, trailing off.

But the next moment, his eyes go wide, and he sets the letters aside, going back to the drawer in a hurry.

"What's wrong?" I ask.

"This desk— the reports told me the fire destroyed everything of value, and I wasn't in a hurry to come revisit this place all burned to ashes, so I never thought to check. But this lower drawer here has a false bottom."

"What for?" Sandy asks as the lot of us gather

around the desk, watching Jon pull one of the side drawers out entirely, pushing past some charred office supplies to open a false bottom.

"Official documents," Jon explains, flashing us a grin. "You know, tax records, receipts for big expenses, that kind of thing. More importantly though, this is where I kept all the letters that moved around that had to do with the foreclosure battle."

"Oh my god, that's perfect," Lila says, stepping forward and helping him start taking out handfuls of letters. "Everyone, take a stack— let's start sifting through all this."

Huddled in a charred, open-air ruin of what used to be a very diligent man's study, we start reading through everything. My stack contains mostly the financial details. I'm impressed that Jon was able to hold the line in the neighborhood for so long— the bank was waving a lot of money at him for this place before they went to foreclosure. He must have known that they were doing something shady and dug his heels in for the sake of the rest of the neighborhood.

"Hey, Cha- Chris, can you come over here and double-check this for me?" Lila asks, sounding reluctant and almost suspicious.

I step over to crouch beside her and look at what she's reading, and she hands it to me. My eyes scan over it, and as they do, I realize why she seemed so stunned by what she was reading.

"What is it?" Sandy asks, looking up at us.

"This…can this be right?" I say, squinting. "It lists the bids that were coming in for the house, and one of them is obviously Ed's, but…it's not Ed's company." I look up and to everyone else. "The company is registered under Lila's name."

"Why would he have his company under Lila's name?" Sandy asks, furrowing her brow.

"I know he wanted me to be his successor, I guess, but that doesn't really explain this…" Lila says, scratching her head.

"Can I see that?" Cass asks, approaching to look at the paper. "I know a site where I can look up public info about registered companies. I learned about it in a business class I had to take, long story."

Cassandra furiously types away at her phone, glancing at the paper every now and then, and I pace with my hands on my hips while we wait with baited breath.

"Okay," Cass says, "this company was registered in Lila's name…not long after she was born, actually. It looks like he set it up as one of those things where, for tax purposes, it's in his child's name until she's old enough to assume full ownership once she reaches a certain age. It's actually not that unusual, for people like him, I mean. In this case, Lila assumes full ownership on her 21st birthday."

"That's…tomorrow," Lila says, looking disoriented.

"There's no way that information is current," I say, shaking my head, not willing to believe something that good so easily. "A guy like Ed covers his basis. He must have had that changed recently."

"I'm not so sure, now that you mention it," Lila says, rubbing her forehead. "He always thinks my birthday is the week before Christmas, not the week before Thanksgiving. If he planned on changing it, he thinks he has a few more months still to go."

"That bastard was using you for some kind of tax scheme and didn't even bother to tell you about it?" Sandy says, going red in the face.

"But if this is current information, that means you'll be the one who runs your dad's business as of tomorrow," I say, barely able to believe it myself.

"And I'll have access to all his records," Lila says, looking at Jon. "I could get any of the info I need to incriminate him!"

I open my mouth to reply.

BANG.

I can see everyone's shocked faces around me, and I watch Jon grab Cassandra and Sandy grab Lila to get down. But I can't hear any of it. All I can hear is the loud, sharp ringing in my ears. I put a hand to an odd feeling on the side of my head, and I feel something warm and sticky.

A bullet just grazed my ear.

I get down at the same time that my hearing starts to come back to me slowly. I hear the shouting of Jon and Shirley as I reach for the pistol I have hidden in my pant leg, and I quickly grab Lila and help her and Sandy get down.

"What the fuck was that?!" Sandy shouts, looking ready to kill a man with her bare hands as Jon helps Cass take cover behind the ruined desk.

"Gunshot!" I bark, and I gesture sharply to the edge of the house. "Get out of the room, take cover behind the foundation!"

"Who shot at us?" Lila shouts as she scoops up a madly barking Henry and shields him with her body.

That's one thing I can guess the answer to before I even look. I turn my eyes to our cars, and I see that we've been snuck up on. There are men heading our way, all of them dressed in black, all of them armed with pistols, all of them trained on us.

"I think your dad's been watching us," I growl before I fire off a couple of shots back at the men.

They must not have expected me to be armed, because one of them goes down immediately, not even taking cover. The others catch on very quickly, though, and soon, they're hurrying into positions behind the cars.

"They're moving, get to cover, now!" I bark at the others, and this time, they listen. Two by two, all of them disappear behind the concrete foundations of the house, and the second they're safe, I start charging in the opposite direction.

Fear means nothing to me anymore. I've faced

the worst the world has to throw at a guy like me, and now, I have the beginnings of something that I care about, right here with me.

I take cover behind what used to be an oven as shots start whizzing overhead and pinging off my rusty barrier. The door of the oven is missing, and I look inside to see a large cast iron skillet sitting inside. I reach in and toss it out from behind the stove to the left, and immediately, shots start hitting it.

At the same time, I lean out from the right side of the oven, and I manage to drop one of the men hiding behind Cass's car. Once he's down, the other guys look over in shock, and I use that distraction to drop another before darting out of cover and running for the living room.

This time, I don't have the benefit of something big and metal to hide me, but I have to keep moving forward. I have to keep them firing at me, away from where the other, unarmed innocents are hiding. These thugs are from Ed Hawthorne, and I know they won't shy away from killing them.

Hell, the feeling in my gut tells me that if they're here, that means Ed has decided he wants no survivors. Lila was standing close to me when that shot grazed my ear. He wouldn't have taken that shot if this hit squad meant to leave anyone alive.

I'm glad we parked so close to the house. I race past the remains of a heavy bookshelf, fake out, and dart back through the front door. I have one more shot left in my gun, and I'm going to make it count. In the meantime, that's not the only weapon I have.

My knife has served me well before, and it will again.

Adrenaline is coursing through me by the time I reach the cars, and I know there's more than one gun barrel trained on me, but I don't care. I couldn't care if I tried. I'm seeing red now, and I'm not about to let a little gunfire stop me.

As I vault over the hood of Sandy's car, I feel a couple of what feel like bee stings in my shoulder and leg, but that can't stop me either. I'm closing in on one of the men, and I hear him swear when he sees 6 and a half feet of big, burly, bearded man lunge at him with a knife in hand. I tackle him to the ground, and by the time his body thuds under me, the knife has sunk into his neck and out the other side.

I rip it out and turn around me to the man standing behind him, and before he can get the shot off, I raise my pistol and fire the last round into his eye.

A third bullet hits my shoulder from behind, but I don't turn around. I dive for the gun in the hands of the man who I just killed, and I wrench it from his dying grasp before spinning around.

I freeze.

The last man standing is much closer than I

anticipated, but he's frozen too. We're at a standoff, and neither of us is willing to move a muscle.

"Drop the gun, and you might live," I growl.

"Tough words for a man losing that much blood," the assassin retorts.

I clench my jaw, feeling the warm ooze down my chest and legs. I'm starting to feel woozy, but I can fight it off…for now. But soon, my injuries are going to catch up to me. I wonder if they hit anything vital.

If I'm already a dead man, I might as well kill this bastard and take him down with me.

Click.

"He said drop the gun."

It's Lila, standing over the body of one of the men I've killed, holding the gun and pointing it at the last assassin. I don't think she knows how to shoot, but at this close a range, that's not a risk any sane man would take.

The mercenary glares me down for a few seconds…then drops his weapon, raising his hands and putting them behind his head.

Sandy immediately races over and snatches the gun, adding to the number of people keeping the man at gunpoint, and I smile.

"Shit, you did great," I say. "You're…great."

"Chains!" Lila shouts, and it's the last thing I see before I look down, see my white shirt drenched in my own blood, and feel myself pass out.

I finally appreciate the quiet, dark, cozy solitude of the comfort of my own room, kneeling on my soft bed…and waiting for the new addition to my daily life.

The black silk blindfold is weightless on my face, but it blocks out any light in the already dim room. My hands are cuffed behind my back, and the cuffs are linked by a thin chain to a collar around my neck. Every time I shift, I'm reminded of the soft, scant, frilly lingerie hugging my body and exposing me like a work of art to the dark room around me.

But there's only one set of eyes that deserves to look at me when I'm all bound up like this.

Chains's heavy footsteps make my body shiver as he comes close to the bed. I can hear him breathing, looking my body up and down and murmuring in soft approval. It has been over a week, and seeing how quickly he recovered from the bullet wounds he took to his muscles has shown me just how powerful and terrifying his body really is.

He told me it was just because he couldn't keep from touching me any longer.

I believe it with all my heart.

"Do you like it?" I breathe in a weak whisper into the darkness as he paces around the bed like a hungry animal, taking in my scent and drinking in my silhouette.

"Bold question," his deep voice rumbles.

He steps close to the bed from behind, and I feel the mattress under me shift as he kneels on it and approaches me. The next moment, his huge, rough hands are running up from my hips to my breasts. He gropes me, feeling their weight and rubbing his fingers around the rich fabric of my lacy bra. I suck in a sharp breath and realize how hard my nipples are when he touches them, even through the bra.

He chuckles and runs his thumbs along the edge of the bra, teasing me gently as he brings his mouth to my neck and breathes on me. His beard tickles my shoulder, and my heart races.

"Do you trust me?" he growls.

"Yes, Daddy," I reply softly, obediently.

"Good girl," he growls, and squeezes my breasts a little harder. "What's the safe word?"

"Pepper," I breathe.

"That's right," he says. "Say that word, and every-thing stops."

He takes hold of my chain and pulls me back by the leash very gently, letting his fingers show how much control over me it gives him. Every time he moves me around, I feel a shiver of delight go through my body. I'm not holding the reins here, he is.

I'm Daddy's plaything, and the thought of that is getting me wet.

"Show me your neck, girl," he commands me.

I bite my lip, hesitating as a devious thought crosses my mind. Instead of yielding immediately, I turn my head away, shying away from his command. I can't help but enjoy testing Daddy's authority. The rebellion gives me a thrilling shiver.

Who am I kidding? I do it because I like the consequences.

I hear a low growl from Chains's chest, and he tugs at my leash in a firm, steady pull that makes me arch my back for him as he unhooks the chain from my cuffs to hold it like a leash.

The next thing I know is the sharp *crack* of his hand against my ass as he spanks me, and I let out a whimpering yelp.

"Feeling disobedient today, pet?" he snarls at me, making me quiver like a leaf. "You know what happens when my little girl doesn't give me what I want."

"I'm sorry, Daddy," I whisper.

He wraps the chain around his fist and guides me back, and he takes one hand away from me. That would be enough of a punishment— denying me pleasure is one of his favorite ways of making me squirm.

But then, I hear the metallic *shink* of a switchblade popping open, and a ripple of excitement runs up my body.

"You know what that sound means, girl," he growls.

I do. He brings the knife to my shoulder, letting the flat of the blade trace over my skin and wander its way down my soft, exposed chest. He drags the tip across the fine lace, and I feel my heart pounding.

"If you don't give me *complete* obedience," he says, gripping my breast with his other hand, "I take something from you. It's too bad. I liked this outfit."

"No, please! I'll be good!"

He brings the knife to where my bra meets between my breasts, and in one swift motion, he cuts it open. I gasp, remembering the price tag, but how casually and ruthlessly he rips it open excites me. He doesn't stop there, either. He brings the knife up to the shoulders and cuts them loose too, then some of the straps at the back. He makes sure I can hear the sound of the expensive fabric ripping as he lets it fall to the sheets in pieces.

He isn't even finished.

"Don't move," he orders, and he puts the dull side of the knife to my stomach.

Slowly, he starts tracing circles, weaving around my belly and working his way to my panties. My heart pounds against my chest, hoping he'll at least leave those— I know how much he likes them. But Daddy's consequences are severe. He expects nothing but complete obedience, and if I want to rebel against that, I have to be punished.

"Are you learning your lesson dove?" his thick, husky voice growls into my ear.

"I deserve this," I affirm, breathing steadily.

"Yes, you do," he says. "You've been a bad girl. You didn't even greet me when I entered the room."

"I'm so sorry, Daddy," I whimper. "I promise, I'll be good."

"That's not enough, sweetie," he says ominously.

On cue, he slides the blade into my panties at the hip, and with one quick slice, the panties are destroyed. He carefully closes the switchblade and removes it from the bed, then takes hold of my panties and tosses them aside. I'm completely naked for him, except for my leash.

"Bend," he commands me.

"Daddy, are you…?"

CRACK!

He spanks me harder this time, and I whimper, hastily bending forward and pushing my ass up into the air for him. My face presses against the soft sheets, and I hear a murmur of approval before his hand gropes my ass. He takes his time, feeling its roundness and testing it with gentle squeezes.

"You make me hard, girl," he growls. "Have you learned your lesson?"

"Yes, Daddy," I plead.

"I don't think you have," he snarls, sliding his hand further down the chain so he can grip my hips with both hands. "But when I'm through with you, you will have."

I feel something thick, hard, and hungry rest between my ass cheeks, pointing toward my back. It's lightly oiled, and it glides between my cheeks, giving me a pulse to show me how lustful his cock is for me. But he's tantalizingly far from my pussy.

Next, his fingers slide around my hip and down toward my clit…but it avoids it, teasing around my puffy lips instead. He dives them deep enough to touch my wetness, and he chuckles.

"You're too eager for what I have to give you, greedy little girl," he taunts me.

"I can't help myself," I whimper, almost apologetically, embarrassed, blushing.

"I know, sweetie," he assures me, stroking me gently. "Don't you worry. Daddy's going to take care of you."

When he says those words, he moves his cock back, and I have just the briefest of moments to get ready before he slides it down between my thighs and into my pussy.

Daddy's thick cock impales me, pushing past my delicate lips with all hits hefty girth and throbbing on its way into my tight cunt. I let out a squeal as the sensation overwhelms me. It's rough and sudden, but I like it that way. No, I love it that way. His cock fills me up and overwhelms me, and that's something I truly love.

His bulging crown grinds all the way through to my g-spot, and immediately, he hoists my hips up to start rutting furiously into them. When Daddy takes what he wants, he takes it hard and fast, and all the anticipation that he's been building up in me starts to threaten to let go immediately. It wells up tighter, as tight as his grip on my hips that I hope will leave a bruise.

He's always so careful, so professional and precise with me that I'd trust him with my life. Trust is the most important part, above all, and my time with Chains only makes me trust him more each day.

He rules me in the bedroom, takes everything from me, sometimes even my breath.

His endless pounding makes me wish I had control of my arms so I could grab the sheets, but no, even that is denied me. I bite down on the pillow, whimpering as I feel myself getting pushed closer to orgasm with every repetitive, deep, thick thrust. My squealing gasps get a higher pitch each time he bucks into me, and I feel myself on the very brink of coming…

…and he stops.

I try to look back at him in protest, but he tugs my chain, chastising me for moving out of line.

"Such a noisy girl," he growls, and I hear the sound of another piece of gear I hadn't noticed until now.

He lets go of my chain, then takes whatever he's holding in both hands and brings it toward my face, lowering it over the front. I get goosebumps when I feel the ball gag on my lips, and I blush harder.

"Take it," he commands me.

I obey promptly, and he fastens it to my head, rendering me silent, no matter what I try.

"Good girl," he rumbles.

He pulls back, making me gasp into the gag, and he picks up the chain again to resume bucking. I feel like a plaything, completely deprived of so much control of my own body. He's so thick and satisfying that I don't want or need anything else— I want to give it all to Chains, let him fill me up and use me and do it all over again, whenever and wherever he wants.

And Daddy's hunger is insatiable.

He thrusts harder and harder, over and over again, and I feel so restrained and comfortable at the same time. It's a delicious prison, and the deeper he goes, the more I can't help but think about that first night he truly did grab me, holding me against his rock-hard body until I lost consciousness.

The thought sends me spiraling, like it always does, and Daddy feels me.

"That's my girl," he growls, getting faster and losing his rhythm second by second. "That's it, come for me. Make me proud."

My groan starts small, but then I feel my body tense up moments before an explosive, over-whelming orgasm wracks my entire body. I can't help but moan and thrash as my body twitches, but Daddy's control is still absolute, even as he starts to let out jets of hot seed into my fertile, wet pussy.

He holds me tight while he pumps his load into me, shot after shot, pushing his dark crown against my g-spot and bathing it in hot, thick come. Daddy empties himself in me, and I feel tears streaming down my eyes in wonderful, emotional release.

I'm dazed by the time it's over. My heart keeps pounding even as Daddy carefully unlocks my hand-cuffs and puts them aside. He massages my wrists gently, then reaches forward and takes the collar off.

"That's a good girl," he coos gently. "You did so good for me."

"Did I make you happy, Daddy?" I breathe, still barely able to wrap my head around how good those words feel to say.

"So happy," he chuckles as he takes the blindfold

off and slowly slides out of me. "You make me a very happy man, Lila.

Once his cock is out of me, he scoops me up into his arms and peppers me with kisses, caressing me gently. His aftercare is the sweetest feeling in the world, and he carries me in his arms bridal-style to the shower, where the hot water soon starts washing us both off and letting us unwind.

I beam up at his wet face, watching his hungry eyes devour me as he pushes his half-mast cock against my overwhelmed pussy. Every day like this reminds me how glad I am I asked him to move in with me on my birthday last week. He's more of a birthday present I ever thought I'd get.

"I love it when you call me Daddy," he purrs, running his fingers through my wet hair.

"You're the only one who deserves me calling him that," I say back, proudly.

Half an hour later, we're dressed and heading downstairs, with me leading the way to the kitchen.

It's Thanksgiving, and the guests are expected to show up within the hour!

"Your mom has the address, right?" Chains asks as I pad into the kitchen and start pulling out pots and pans to start on everything that isn't already in progress.

"Yep!" I chime happily, still getting used to refer-ring to my mom in casual conversation. "She'll be a little late, she said."

Henry trots up to me and circles around my legs before going to Chains and letting him pet him while Chains turns the TV on. Thanksgiving is normally small, but this year, I have Cassandra, my mom, and Chains's entire gang (minus Ryder, who Chains sent to go be with his own family) to feed. We have our work cut out for us, including Chains, who it turns out isn't half bad in the kitchen.

"Shit," Chains chuckles as the TV plays, "Lila, come check this out."

I walk into the living room and see a familiar sight on the screen that makes me gasp, but the next moment, I smile.

Dad is getting arrested on the news, being led out of his own office building—*my* office building now—and into a police car. The news anchor is listing the charges against him, which are numerous: fraud, tax evasion, attempted murder, arson, and many more.

The mercenary we captured was not the team's leader, and it didn't take him long to start spilling all the secrets he'd gathered about my father. Between that and the evidence we gathered from the house and the documents I seized as rightful owner of my father's company, my father was going away for a very, very long time. It turns out there are a lot of lawyers who have been dying to get their shot at him for a while.

"That'll make it a lot easier to start using his

assets to clean up the evil he's done over the years," I say.

There's no easy way to watch your father get arrested, no matter how unquestionably horrible he is, but I'm glad for it, especially because I know how much good I can do.

"I think we have all the time in the world for that," Chains says, turning and approaching me with that big smile I love so much on his face.

"We do," I agree, meeting him halfway and feeling his arms go around my waist. "And I might just need a team of big, strong construction workers to make some of it happen."

"I might just know where to get one of those," he chuckles.

He bends down and kisses me, and I feel filled with a special kind of domestic bliss and love for the huge, terrifying man in front of me who has so much power over me yet all the respect and adoration in the world. We belong to each other, and from here on out, it's us against the world.

And I wouldn't have it any other way.

"Now," he says as he breaks the kiss, smiling. "Let's make a turkey that our new family will *remember*."

~

Thank you so much for reading! I hope you enjoyed <3 If you have a moment, please leave a review. Other readers are dying to know what you thought.

I have plenty more bad boy romance for you, so make sure you check out my other books on the next couple of pages, and sign up for my newsletter to be notified when I have a new release on the way!

~Alexis Abbott

Killing For Her

Abducted

Stepbrothers:

Ruthless

Criminal

Standalones:

Betting on Love

Hunter's Baby

I Hired A Hitman

Vegas Boss

Rock Hard Bodyguard

Innocence For Sale: Jane

Redeeming Viktor

Romance:

Falling for her Boss (Novella)

Most Wanted: Lilly (Novella)

Bound as the World Burns (SFF)

Erotic Thriller:

The Dangerous Men Series:

The Narrow Path

Strayed from the Path

Path to Ruin

ABOUT THE AUTHOR

Alexis Abbott is a Wall Street Journal & USA Today bestselling author who writes about bad boys protecting their girls! Pick up her books today if you can't resist a bad boy who is a good man, and find yourself transported with super steamy sex, gritty suspense, and lots of romance.

She lives in beautiful St. John's, NL, Canada with her amazing husband.

facebook.com/abbottauthor

twitter.com/abbottauthor

instagram.com/alexisabbottauthor

bookbub.com/authors/alexis-abbott

pinterest.com/badboyromance

youtube.com/AlexisAbbott

ACKNOWLEDGMENTS

Thank you to my amazing Patrons. I'm constantly humbled and grateful for your support.

Ramona Cabrera
Melissa Hedrick
Virginia Swanson
Dawn Daughenbaugh
Don Doss
Stacie Currie

If you'd like to join them — and get my ebooks or paperbacks — you can find me here on Patreon.
https://www.patreon.com/alexisabbott